# AZAAN & Jayda

## Fallin' For A Haitian Hitta

# 2

A NOVEL BY

# NATISHA RAYNOR

**Royalty Publishing House** is now accepting manuscripts from aspiring or experienced urban romance authors!

**WHAT MAY PLACE YOU ABOVE THE REST:**

Heroes who are the ultimate book bae: strong-willed, maybe a little rough around the edges but willing to risk it all for the woman he loves.

Heroines who are the ultimate match: the girl next door type, not perfect - has her faults but is still a decent person. One who is willing to risk it all for the man she loves.

The rest is up to you! Just be creative, think out of the box, keep it sexy and intriguing!

If you'd like to join the Royal family, send us the first 15K words (60 pages) of your completed manuscript to submissions@royaltypublishing-house.com

# SYNOPSIS

Azaan's relationship with Vickie is crumbling, and he no longer has to wonder who he should be with. The decision is made for him when he discovers that Vickie is still keeping secrets from him. When she calls on Azaan to clean up one of her messes that turned deadly, it's then that he realizes that he doesn't really know her. Azaan is ready to risk it all and be with Jayda, but she's still grieving Biggs' death and still running from Azaan. Will he grow tired of chasing a woman that doesn't want to be chased? Azaan is also keeping a secret, a secret that if Jayda finds out, she's sure to hate him for.

It's clear to anyone with eyes that Azaan makes Jayda happy. No matter how much she tries to fight it, he's it for her. Jayda tries to keep herself busy by enrolling back in law school but not even that changes the fact that her mind has suddenly become consumed with Azaan. Just when she decides to put her guard down, Jayda finds out that Azaan has been keeping a huge secret from her. One that could alter their relationship forever.

# PREVIOUSLY...

## AZAAN

I drove towards my club with a grin on my face like an idiot. Jayda was a handful indeed. I was digging her little nonchalant attitude, but I knew even the hardest of women could be broken. It would be a challenge that would stroke my ego for sure if I made the impossible happen, but I was going to leave it alone. I wasn't going to pursue her relentlessly when I wasn't even sure of what the fuck I had going on. The situation with Vickie was threatening to stress me out for real. In my opinion, I'd been really cool about the situation. I was pissed, but that was to be expected. I was still just chilling though. My moves hadn't been too drastic. I loved my aunt with everything in me, but her fuck ass son was gon' die. Prison was the safest place for him to be at the moment, and he didn't even know it.

On one hand, I wanted to say what Vickie did was unforgivable, but I loved her dumb ass, and I needed to be sure before I walked away from us. Jayda had nothing to do with it because had she not been in the picture, I'd still be feeling the exact same way. Vickie violated. I couldn't even be too mad that her initial intentions were to use me. That's a lot of women's intention when they get with a nigga, but got damn. After she so called fell in love with me she couldn't even put me up on game and let me know how foul my cousin was. This dude lowkey hated me and my girl knew, and she didn't say a bitch ass thing. That's what had me giving her the side eye, and she still wouldn't have told me if I hadn't caught her. That shit almost had me feeling like I was sleeping with the enemy. For real.

I was going to work at the club for about three hours and then do my final pick up from the trap. I had been working hard every day. I was pretty confident that the club was going to do well but even so, the first few months would bring me the money back that I put into it. I expected it to take anywhere from three to six months for the club to really start seeing a profit. The drug business was great, so I had the time to wait for the club to do what I needed it to do. Fahan was going to be my equal partner. It meant nothing to me that all the money to start the club came from me. Once I started seeing a profit, we would split it fifty-fifty no matter what. I just wanted him to come home and go down the right path. Just get legal money and enjoy life out here with his girl.

All the hiring had been done. The club had ten bad ass strippers. A few of them were from out of town, and they assured me they had no issues with driving an hour or more each night to dance. I had also hired four bartenders with amazing bodies, six cocktail waitresses, and I had kitchen staff. There were two females to work the door and six bouncers. I also knew that the money for the staff minus the strippers may have to come from my pockets until the club started seeing a profit. I knew all of this going in, and I was prepared for it. I had over a half million dollars of drug money stashed so that no matter what, I could live and pay my staff even if the club started out doing slow business. Anybody going into business thinking they were going to make money right away was tripping.

I was about my paper, and I didn't let too many things distract me from that, so while I was handling business at the club, my mind wasn't on Vickie or Jayda, but when I got in my car and saw that I had a text from Jayda, a nigga smirked. I read over her address as I knew that dealing with her was like playing with fire, but I was down for the adventure.

The moment I pulled in front of the trap I knew that something was wrong. I saw a figure running through the front yard, and I heard a gunshot and the figure instantly fell forward. I couldn't see if it was one of my people or not, but I grabbed my gun from underneath the seat. Just as I was about to place my hand on the door handle, a beat up old car sped past me fast as hell. Something told me that car had something to do with what just went down at my trap. Torn between going and staying, I made the split decision to follow the car. The car was sitting at a stop sign as I approached. I hopped out of my car and ran up to the car.

Inside, a woman was screaming, and a white dude sat in the passenger seat slumped over. His shirt was saturated with blood. The female was so fixated on him that she didn't even notice that I was up on the car. When I yanked the door open, she whirled around with wide eyes, and when she saw my 9mm pointed in her face, she gasped. My brows furrowed from recognition. It was fuckin' Liah.

She drew back in the seat as far as she could go. "Please don't hurt me," she cried.

That bitch tried to rob my trap. Having no regard for the fact that she was Jayda's sister, I squeezed the trigger of my gun and got the fuck out of dodge before her body even slumped all the way over. I got back in my car and busted a U-turn at the same time that Nas was calling my phone.

"I'm right here," I answered breathlessly. "What went down?"

"We gon' fam. Body in the front yard. We cleared everything out and got the fuck away from there. We're going to have to find a new location."

"All my people good?" I inquired.

"We straight my nigga. Fuck boys didn't get nothing but some hot slugs."

I breathed a sigh of relief. "Bet. Just go lay low. We'll handle all the particulars tomorrow."

"Bet."

I raced home so I could take a shower. Feeling not one ounce of remorse for what I'd done, I wondered how long it would take to get word to Jayda that her sister was shot. I didn't even know if the bitch was dead, but if I hurried, maybe I'd have time to still fuck Jayda before she got the call. If I was there when she got the call, I'd also be able to find out if Liah was dead or alive. If she wasn't dead, I had no problem finishing the job at a later time. She was a lowlife ass fiend. Shorty was better off dead anyway.

# 1

## JAYDA

I stared at my reflection in the mirror. Dressed in nothing but crème satin, floral print shorts that were a tad bit too small and a matching camisole, I was pleased with what I saw staring back at me. I was damn near bursting out of the shorts, and I was scared if I moved wrong I would. I didn't take them off though because they made my thighs look juicy and edible. I knew why I invited Azaan over, and he did too. Beating around the bush wasn't necessary. In fact, it was childish and stupid. We could skip the small talk and get right down to business as soon as he walked in the door for all I cared.

I grabbed some clear gloss off my dresser and moisturized my lips. I had on no make-up, and I smelled of soap and lotion. Plain and simple looking. Just ready to be fucked by a man that was so handsome he literally made my mouth water. As I continued to ogle my own reflection, my eyes fell on the tattoo of Biggs' face on my arm, and my eyes quickly darted away. I couldn't look at him now. I didn't really feel guilt, but I didn't want to stare at him. The detail of my tattoo was insane, and sometimes it really felt as if Biggs was staring up at me.

My doorbell rang, and my heartrate increased just a bit. I wasn't sure why I was nervous. Afterall, this was what I wanted. I already knew that it was going to be good. I walked to the front door and looked out of the peephole to make sure it was who I was expecting. Azaan was looking to the left of him but I could see the side of his face. Even that was handsome. I opened the door and greeted him with a small smile. His eyes quickly roamed over my body, and I saw a light flicker in his eyes.

"What's up?" he asked, stepping inside.

It was my turn to observe him from head to toe and as usual, he was looking like a snack. Even dressed super casual in gray Nike sweats and a gray, white, and red Nike shirt, he made me lick my lips with anticipation of being wrapped in his muscular arms.

"Not much. I see you wore your thot outfit," I joked, and he let out a light chuckle.

"Ahhhh, you trying to play me. Well, that's what you treat me like. You only want me for the D." He shrugged, and I gave him an amused smirk. He was right, so what was I supposed to say?

"You want something to drink?"

"I want you." Azaan invaded my personal space, and we stared at each other for a few moments. With bated breath I waited for him to make a move. My heart skipped a few beats and finally, he covered my lips with his and snaked his tongue into my mouth. He kneaded my ass cheeks with his hands as we kissed and my nipples hardened, poking through the thin satin material of the camisole.

I felt his manhood poking me through his sweats. I sucked gently on his bottom lip, then grabbed his hands and led him to my bedroom. As soon as we were over the threshold, Azaan took control. He pulled my too tight camisole over my head and admired my body briefly before placing soft kisses on my stomach and then hungrily devouring my breasts. I moistened my lips with my tongue and closed my eyes as I enjoyed the feel of his tongue rolling over my nipples. After removing his sweats, he pulled a condom from the pocket, removed his shirt and used his body to push mine down onto the bed.

I loved kissing Azaan. His mouth always tasted minty. His hands explored my body as our tongues danced and he gently pushed his dick into me causing me to moan into his mouth. After breaking our kiss, he stared into my eyes long enough for me to notice that there was something there. I couldn't quite read it though. I didn't want to accept it, but I lowkey knew that the connection that I had with Azaan was more than sex. He didn't have one characteristic or personality trait that I'd seen that I didn't like. He was a whole mood. Sweet, laid back, calm, and about his business. The way he took his time with me, the way he complimented me, the way he fell back and let me decide how I wanted to do things, it struck a chord with me. But as I predicted long ago, I'd never find another man like Biggs. For all the good qualities that Azaan had, there was one deciding factor in how seriously I could take him. His, whatever she was that showed up at his place that night. I didn't even care to ask about her.

"Shit," he whispered in my ear as he grinded in and out of me.

I spread my legs as wide as I could. "You feel so fuckin' good," I moaned as he stirred my middle passionately. I was trying to make myself savor the moment. I was telling myself that this could possibly be the last time that I ever had sex with Azaan. For as good as he felt, I didn't need to become addicted to him. Thoughts of him already invaded my thoughts entirely too much.

Azaan flipped me over, and I reached behind me and spread my ass cheeks open for him. We moaned simultaneously as he slid back into me. As soon as he slid his finger into my ass my body bucked slightly, and my pussy muscles contracted like crazy. With his hands gripping my waist, Azaan pounded into me savagely as my honey poured down my thighs. I was super wet, and when I started throwing my ass back at him matching his rhythm, he let out a guttural moan.

Cupping one of my breasts in my hand, I pulled my lips in, closed my mouth, and enjoyed him pounding in and out of me. "I'm 'bout to bust," he grunted as he grabbed a handful of my hair and gently pulled my head back.

"Ummmmm," I moaned as my clit swelled. The closer he got to an orgasm, the harder he pounded into me, and I had an orgasm of my own building.

"Ahhhhhhhh." I buried my face in my pillow as waves of pleasure rippled through my stomach. My toes curled, and I gripped the sheets as a second orgasm rocked my body.

"Fuuckkk," Azaan hissed as he came with me, and his seeds shot into the condom that he was wearing.

When he pulled out of me, we were both quiet and out of breath. My chest heaved up and down as I went to the bathroom to clean up, then I brought out a warm, soapy rag. Azaan watched me from his sitting position on my bed as I cleaned his dick off. Sex was just the night cap that I needed because I was already thinking about snuggling up underneath my covers and going to sleep. My cell phone rang, and I handed the rag to Azaan so he could finish the task. I saw that my mom was calling, and I started to just call her back when he left, but something told me to answer it.

"Hey Mommy."

"Jayda, I just got a call from Janice's daughter that works in the emergency room." Janice lived down the street from my mother and was a retired district attorney. When she found out I was going to law school, she started gushing over me and invited me over often. "It seems Liah was brought in by ambulance almost an hour ago. Someone shot her. She was unconscious and taken right into emergency surgery. Kimmy was on break when she first got there, but as soon as she recognized Liah, she called her mother so her mother could call me. I'm on my way to the hospital now."

My mother sounded weary and stressed, but she wasn't crying and that surprised me. She'd shed a lot of tears over Liah for much less than her being shot. Maybe she was in shock, but I really didn't see how. When Liah first got in the streets bad, my mother used to make herself physically ill worrying about Liah. She didn't get any sleep at night, and she barely ate. After a while my father put his foot down and told her she had to stop it. Liah was going to do what Liah wanted to do, and my father refused to let my mother stress herself to death behind it. He told her to give it to God and to let it go. It had gotten to a point where anytime my phone rang late at night, I always hoped that I wasn't getting a call saying that Liah had overdosed or gotten killed. Was this the call that I'd feared for years?

"Which hospital? I'll be right there." Liah and I had our issues, but me not going to the hospital wasn't even an option.

"Carolina's Medical Center."

"Okay." I ended the call and walked over to my dresser to find something to throw on. My eyebrows were furrowed low, and worry had my face crumpled as if in slight pain.

"What's wrong?" Azaan came out of the bathroom as I pulled my top drawer open and grabbed a pair of leggings.

"That was my mom. Liah got shot, and she's in surgery." Just that fast it was as if a lump formed in my throat and chopped off the last part of the last word I spoke. My hands were trembling. I was scared. More scared than I'd been in a long time. Since the night Biggs died in my arms.

Having someone that you love take their last breath in your arms does something to you. It hardened me just a bit. The average things that hurt the average person didn't affect me the same. It took a lot to make me cry because in my opinion, I'd been through damn near the worst. The only thing that would hurt more than losing Biggs would be losing my parents or a child that I'd birthed. Don't get me wrong, I mourned my miscarriage, but I knew the sorrow had to be greater when you lose a child that you've actually birthed into the world. If I lost Liah, it would no doubt hurt, but with the life she lived and the things that she'd done, I wasn't shocked with what happened. I just wanted her to get herself together and stop stressing my mother out. If it wasn't too late.

"Damn, I'm sorry to hear that. Do you need me to drive you to the hospital?" I pulled my leggings on and absentmindedly grabbed a shirt from the second drawer. My mouth was dry.

"No, I'm good. Thank you so much for offering." Once I pulled the shirt over my head, I gave him a tight smile. "I'll be okay."

His eyes darted back and forth across my face. Genuine concern filled his eyes. "Are you sure? I don't mind."

"Yes, I'm sure. Thank you." I kissed him on the cheek and then slipped my feet into some slides.

We headed for my front door, and Azaan wrapped his arms around me and gave me the tightest hug. "Call me," he stated before pecking me on the lips and leaving.

I stood there and took three deep breaths. I needed to focus so I could drive to the hospital. "Focus," I coached myself in a voice just above a whisper.

I could only hope that whatever Liah had gotten herself into didn't kill her. Lord knows my mother wouldn't be able to take it.

## 2

# DIOR

"Damn, I like that long ass blonde hair," Fahan stated as he licked his lips. "Every time I see you that shit different. I like that shit."

It was safe to say that my twenty-two-inch blonde lacefront wig was a hit with my man. "Yeah for the show, I switch it up every other day. This is a wig." I hoped he couldn't tell that I was nervous. It had been a few days since I had sex with Marshon, and with a sober mind guilt was eating my ass alive.

I actually woke up the next day and cried but crying wouldn't erase what I'd done. I took drugs, and I made a dumb ass decision. All of the pep talks that I tried to give myself weren't working. I told myself that Fahan would never find out, but that didn't take the guilt away. He was looking at me with nothing but love, desire, and respect, and I'd performed all kinds of sexual acts with someone that I barely even knew. I felt like queen of the sluts.

"How is it going? Everything still cool?" he asked as he used his thumb to stroke the back of my hand lightly.

"It's straight. I really don't like one of those bitches, but I try to think about what you said. I don't want to be on TV looking like a straight up hood rat. I'm trying to come off as business minded and not on the dumb shit. I want to make you proud." I damn near choked off the last sentence. My body grew warm and my palms were sweaty. Had I known cheating would make me feel like that, I never would have done it.

"I'm already proud of you baby, and I mean that shit. You worked so hard holding shit down when I first went away. I know you hated your job, but you got up every morning and went to work because you knew you had to do what you had to do. When I come home, I got you baby. I swear I do. You're not going to want for shit. How you feel about marrying me?"

My eyes damn near popped out of my head. I'd never heard Fahan talk about marriage. I wasn't even sure he was the marriage type. "Married? When?"

"Like next month. I know I don't have a lot of time left, but I want to show you how much I appreciate you. You and my brother are all I have in this world, and when I come home, I promise to make the both of you proud. I'm coming home a changed man. We can get married in here and then after I've been managing the club for a year, we can have a big wedding."

Fat tears spilled over my eyelids and rolled down my cheeks. My dumb ass could never commit a crime because as soon as I got in the interrogation room, I'd get to sweating bullets and crying. I loved Fahan so much, and I was so mad at myself for doing him wrong. His face crumpled with confusion.

"Why you crying ma?"

I sniffed. "I love you too, and I just want you to come home. Of course I'll marry you." I didn't deserve to be Fahan's wife, but I for sure wasn't going to tell him no.

Shit, I did hold him down for over a year. It's not like I was never a good girlfriend to him. I just slipped up one night and did some dumb shit. God was on my side a little bit because Marshon was out of town doing some shows, and I'd only been filming with the ladies. I hadn't even seen him since the day after we had sex, and I was glad. The sex was good as fuck, but I wouldn't be doing it again. I just wanted to put the entire ordeal behind me and focus on my man.

A huge smile stretched across Fahan's face. "Word? I just gotta get permission from the Chaplin, but that won't be a problem. Pick a date next month so you can become Mrs. Cezar."

"My birthday is on the tenth. What about that?" I asked in a weak voice.

He smiled like an excited kid on Christmas. "Perfect."

* * *

"You can't sulk all night Dior, damn. It's over. You did what you did, and you can't take it back. Unless you run your mouth, which would be dumb as fuck of you to do, then how will he ever find out? Charge the shit to the game, and stop being a cry baby. Come out with me tonight," Nico whined.

I let out an exasperated breath because I knew he wasn't going to leave me alone. Plus, he was right. Sulking wasn't going to change shit. All I could do was hope that Fahan never found out about my indiscretion. I don't care how guilty I felt, I was never going to confess. The only other people that knew were Marshon and Nico, and Marshon's ass better not say shit. He wouldn't anyway if he loved his life because Fahan would most definitely body his ass. I wasn't even worried about Nico snitching. We knew all of each other's deepest, darkest secrets. Like aside from the nigga that gave it to him and Nico, I was the only other person that knew Nico had herpes. I'd never breathed a word of it to a soul. When he found out he had it five years ago, he came to me crying and devastated. Nico was so sad behind that shit I damn near thought he was going to commit suicide.

It'd been years though, and he took his medication every day, so he rarely had outbreaks. He said his last one had been more than a year ago and even then, he said he only got like two bumps. According to him the first outbreak was the worst and the most painful. I didn't acknowledge any of what Nico said.

"Oh, I forgot to tell you. The producers said I can film with a friend on

Friday. They want me to pop up on Marshon after one of his out of town shows and make him talk to me," I stated in a solemn voice.

Nico jumped up off the couch like his ass was on fire and started twerking. "Yesssssss, I knew you wouldn't forget about a bitch. They may as well be prepared to give me a spin off show because I'm going to be everything. The flare that this show needs is on the way baby."

I smiled and shook my head at his dramatic ass. That was Nico. I rarely ever saw him down. The dude was always too hype about everything. I really thought he needed meds, but then again, nah he didn't. It's a blessing to always be in good spirits because Lord knows in the last year, I'd done enough sulking for three people. First it was because I missed my man, and now it was because I cheated on my man and I felt bad about it. I was so lost in my thoughts that I hadn't even noticed that Nico had disappeared from the room until he walked over to where I was sitting on the couch and stuck a red plastic cup in my face.

"Drink up and get up! Stop sulking. Let's go have fun," he stomped his foot and whined like a damn child.

I frowned up my face at him. "Uh unn, you too damn big to be acting like that." I curled my upper lip and snatched the cup from him. "No grown man your size should ever do that," I scolded him, meaning every word.

"And no grown woman your size should be sitting up pouting over something you did that Fahan will never even find out about. So you got some dick? Good for you. If you were locked up that man would have held you down to the fullest in the form of money, phone calls, and visits, but baby, don't you for one second get to thinking that he would have kept that dick in his boxers, because he wouldn't have. We need sex to survive. Damn, shake it off sis."

He was right. I was tired of sulking and I was for sure tired of him alternating between pouting and giving me motivational speeches. I tossed my head back and drank the shot of tequila that he'd so graciously poured me. "Ughhhh." I frowned up my face and licked the remnants off my lips.

I stood up, turned on the smart TV and put some Pandora on so we could get dressed to go out. "Yes bitch." Nico started twerking again. He found any reason to shake his ass.

I headed for my bedroom so I could find something to wear before I got in the shower. I hadn't figured out what I was wearing before Nico walked back in the room and handed me more liquor. "I was not playing. Tonight is going to be a lituation."

I chuckled and took the cup from Nico. I drowned my sorrows in alcohol plenty of nights after Fahan went away, so I knew liquor didn't make me do anything that I might end up regretting. I just had to stay away from drugs. After I drank the shot, I decided on a simple black catsuit to wear out. Being that I was on TV I tried to save every fly thing I had for the show. I refused to be on television looking just any kind of way. Especially when I was surrounded by women that wore everything designer down to the headbands on their hair. I'm not ugly at all so with the right accessories, I could make a $20 sundress look fly, but still. I'd be lying if I said I wasn't ready to really start getting money and step my game up.

Even when Fahan was getting money, I was happy wearing PINK, Polo, True Religion, etc. He wasn't a king pin or anything but with his money and the job I had, I always looked nice and kept my hair done. This shit was on a different level though. The women on this reality show had gorgeous homes, foreign cars, and their careers were already established. Then there was me. Just out here trying to figure out life.

Just as I was heading for the bathroom, the doorbell rang. I wondered if Nico had invited anyone over. When I stepped out of my room, I strained my ears over the music, and I heard water running in the main bathroom, so I knew he was in the shower. Once I reached the door, I looked out of the peephole and saw Azaan. I wondered why he always popped up without calling. Probably trying to see if he could catch me doing some shit, but I'd never bring a man to the apartment that Fahan was coming to once he was released from jail. I opened the door with a smile, hoping to let him know that him popping up wasn't a problem.

"Hey Azaan."

"What up? I tried to call you, but your joint was going straight to voicemail."

My eyes widened in surprise. "Really? How long have you been trying to call me?" I turned my back before he could even answer and began scanning the living room for my cell phone. My dumb ass had been sulking so hard, I hadn't even noticed that my battery died.

He stepped inside of the apartment. "About an hour."

"Shit," I hissed as I scooped the phone up from the couch and saw that it was indeed dead. I looked at the watch on my wrist. "Fuuckkk, the phones are going to cut off in less than thirty minutes. I hope Fahan hasn't been trying to call me." I rushed over to the charger that was plugged in by my end table and connected my phone. "I'm sorry." I looked over at Azaan. "My mind has been all over the place."

"It's not a problem. Chill. Take a deep breath. I just came by to give you some more money. You did quit your job, so I have to make sure you're good until my brother gets home. You been good?" he asked as he pulled some money from his pocket.

"Yes, I have. Thank you so much for all that you've done for me. I really appreciate it. Fahan has been happier since I've been visiting him every week."

Azaan handed me the money that he'd just counted out. "I know, and that was the objective, so mission accomplished. If you need anything be sure to let me know."

"I will. Thank you."

"Oh, damn I almost forgot." Azaan snapped his fingers. He slid something out of his pocket and smiled at me. "Bruh said y'all getting married."

A soft gasp escaped my lips as I looked down at the blue velvet ring box in his hands. No Fahan didn't. I guess I looked super shocked because Azaan chuckled. "Aye, my brother might be on lock, but he has me. No way I was letting him get married without doing his shorty right." He handed me the box, as my heart pounded profusely in my chest.

"Thank you so much. I really didn't expect this. I would have married him without a ring. That stuff doesn't matter to me," I stated honestly.

"I know you would have, and he knows it too. That's why he proposed to you. Thank you for making my brother happy." Azaan looked sincere, and that added on to my feelings of guilt.

"You're welcome." I smiled as I walked him to the door.

Once he was gone, I leaned up against the door and closed my eyes. I felt like shit! For the life of me, I couldn't understand how people cheated on their significant other frequently. It wasn't a good feeling. Guilt had engulfed itself around me like a blanket, and it refused to let me go. Slowly, I lifted the lid on the box and tears clouded my vision as I stared down at the gorgeous canary yellow diamond in a white gold setting. It wasn't huge, but it was nice, and I knew out the gate, the diamond was real. I used to work in a jewelry store right before I met Fahan, so if I had to guess, I'd say the ring cost around $3,000, and that wasn't a small amount of money at all.

I prayed that my feelings of guilt would pass. I just tried to look at it on the bright side. The love of my life was coming home in a few months, and I was going to be his wife. As long as I didn't mess up again, everything would be okay.

# 3

# VICKIE

"**G**irl, what in the hell is wrong with you? I may as well be talking to myself," my sister Vittoria exclaimed as I snapped my head in her direction.

We were out eating lunch, and I'd been distracted the entire time. I had barely touched my food. At first, I wanted to keep my problems with Azaan a secret, but the more days that passed, I wanted to tell someone. I needed to tell someone. Who better than my sister?

"I'm sorry. I have a lot on my mind. Azaan and I are on the outs. He's never been this mad at me before. I really messed up," I stated in a voice full of fear. I picked up my wine goblet as Vittoria peered at me with curious eyes.

"Well what in the hell did you do?"

I shook my head lightly, the disappointment in myself evident. "Some dumb shit. I've been sneaking behind his back sending his cousin Meer money, and visiting him while he was locked up."

Recognition flickered in Vittoria's eyes. "Meer that you met years ago at the club?" My sister had a good ass memory. I'm sure she also remembered him because he came around for a few months after we met.

I nodded my head. I knew she would be full of questions, so I went ahead and broke the story down to her. By the time I was done, her mouth was hanging open in shock. "Vickie! Girl…" She was speechless, and that was a first for my sister. She just stared at me while I assumed she was trying to process the situation. "This is bad," she finally assessed.

I chortled. "Tell me about it. Azaan is pissed, and he has a right to be, but I need him to forgive me. To make matters worse, Meer's bitch ass is out of prison, and he popped up at the house the other day." Tears filled my eyes.

Vittoria raised her eyebrows so high, I'm surprised they didn't disappear into her hairline. "You have to do something about this. Meer is testing Azaan's gangster. He must not know how much of a fool Azaan is." Vittoria's tone was laced with worry.

"They're cousins, so I'm sure he knows. His dumb ass just doesn't give a damn. He's still asking me for money, and I don't know what to do. I don't have money of my own like that, and I can't give that man Azaan's money. I've been disloyal enough. I'm telling you the only thing keeping Azaan from never speaking to me again is Aheem, and had we not gotten a blood test after Aheem was born, he'd probably be doubting my son." I was worried and I wasn't trying to front about it.

*"What the fuck are you doing here?" I snapped at Meer. The sight of his smug face repulsed me.*

*A wide grin spread across his sleazy face. "Is that any way to greet an old friend? Man you and Azaan are living like royalty. Got damn," he marveled as he looked around my home. "I can't even imagine what this crib cost, and this furniture is some straight up rich people shit. Cuz came up something lovely, and you're right here reaping the benefits huh? Seems to me you did exactly what I set you out to do, it just took a while. Now, I want my cut."*

*"You are fuckin' insane! Azaan is my boyfriend and the father of my child. I will not take his money and give it to you. He already knows about us. He went through my phone, so the cover is blown. If I were you, I'd lay low because he's out for blood. The moment he lays eyes on you, the shit is a wrap," I gloated. The fear in Meer's eyes almost made me giggle. After*

*all the hell he'd put me through, he had the nerve to look scared. Even though I was scared to death that Azaan wouldn't forgive me, it made me feel almost good to know that Meer couldn't threaten me any longer that he was going to tell him.*

*"He found out and you didn't tell me? What did he say?"*

*I jerked my head back and frowned up my face. "Why would I tell you? I don't owe you anything, and I'm tired of telling you that. My relationship is on the rocks because of your greedy, envious, miserable ass. I no longer have to give you shit out of fear because my worst fear came true. It's been bad for me, but it's gon' be worse for you. Azaan is furious. Nigga are you sweating?" I asked as I squinted my eyes and tried to get a better look at the small beads of sweat that were forming on Meer's forehead. I let out a loud and boisterous laugh. "I know yo' tough ass ain't scared." I placed one hand on my chest and had a good, hearty laugh at his expense, and he didn't like it.*

*Meer stepped forward and grabbed my arm. "I'd shut the fuck up if I were you. There isn't shit funny about this situation. I ain't scared of a soul and if Azaan wants gun play, we can take it there. Just know this. He's not superhuman, and he bleeds like me. You can either give me enough money to leave town with, or me and him can run into each other and shoot it out. You just better hope he's not the one that leaves the scene in a body bag. Think about it. You have three days to come up with $25,000, or whatever happens between me and ya man, happens." He glared into my eyes with his face contorted into a scowl. After a brief stare down, he let me go and walked away.*

Every time I thought about his threat, it sent chills down my spine. Azaan wasn't a punk by far. He was the furthest thing from a punk that anyone could ever get, but one thing Meer said rang true. Azaan wasn't superhuman. If somehow Meer caught him off guard, it was very possible that he could take Azaan's life, and that thought terrified me. It was sad that Meer had such hatred in his heart for his blood cousin all because Azaan succeeded in life and Meer hadn't. That was some sick shit. I drained the wine from my glass and flagged the waitress down for a to-go box. It was the second day, and I hadn't even made up my mind whether or not I was going to actually give Meer the money. Azaan was already pissed with me. I didn't want to call him and even utter Meer's name, but keeping secrets from him was what got me in a messed up predicament in the first place. I just didn't know what to do.

"Sis, how are you going to handle this?" Vittoria asked me the one question that I didn't know the answer to.

I thought about the money that I had in the bank. Money that I was able to save over the years because Azaan took care of my every need. I had a little over $17,000 saved, and I didn't want to drain my bank account for Meer's dumb ass. But on the other hand, if it meant him not bothering Azaan, then it was worth it. I made up my mind that I was going to get Meer out of my hair, and then I was going to get my man back. Whoever the bitch was in North Carolina that he was dealing with better not get used to his ass because he was coming back to me and Aheem, and I didn't give a damn what I had to do to make it happen.

# 4

## JAYDA

"Y ou busy?" That deep baritone voice did something to me.

I leaned back in my chair and glanced out of the window. The more I tried to tell myself that all I wanted from Azaan was dick, the more my subconscious tried to prove to me that wasn't true. If it was all about the D, I wouldn't daydream about him all throughout the day. If it was all about the D, I wouldn't smile every time he called, texted, or sent me flowers. I was intrigued and no matter how much I denied it, it didn't change that fact. Maybe there was enough room in my heart to care for another man, but I wasn't sure how I felt about that. Especially since I didn't even really know Azaan's back story.

"Not at the moment."

"Cool. I was wondering if I could take you to lunch."

Just as I parted my lips to speak, he appeared like a magical Don. He rounded the corner and opened the door to my place of business, eyes locked on me. He was dressed casually in denim shorts and a regular tee, but he still looked like a million bucks. I resisted the urge to lick my lips as I took the phone away from my ear. I stared at him in awe as he neared my desk. Biting my bottom lip, I suppressed a smile.

"And what if I'd been busy?"

"Then I would have waited for you to be done."

"And what if I had said no?"

He actually looked as if he was pondering what I'd said. As if me saying no to him had never entered his mind. "Nah, don't think that would have happened."

I giggled. "You're a very confident man."

"I am. How is your sister?" he asked; his expression turned serious.

I sighed. "Still in a medically induced coma. There's swelling in her brain and slight bleeding. All I know is that she was found in a car with a white boy and a few streets over, another guy had been dumped in the road. The police seem to think the two are connected. My sister is the only one that isn't dead, but we won't know what happened until she wakes up. If she wakes up."

"She's gonna be alright." Azaan looked up as my co-worker came from the back. "So you're free to go grab a bite?" He looked back over at me.

That time I didn't try to hide my smile. "I guess I can spare an hour. It's your lucky day."

"Indeed it is."

Azaan and I ended up walking to a soul food spot a few doors down. He placed his hand on the small of my back and held the door open for me. We were seated right away, and I decided not to beat around the bush. "So the woman that came to your home that night. Is she your girlfriend?"

Azaan looked directly into my eyes. He didn't look away, shift in his seat, or appear nervous. "She's my son's mother." It was then that I realized just how much I *didn't* know about Azaan. I had never asked too much personal information, and he'd never volunteered it. "When I first came to North Carolina, she was my girl. We've since had a few issues, and I honestly at this point don't know what we are. I'm trying to sort it all out."

I didn't respond immediately because the waitress came over and took our orders. Once we were done with that, I spoke. "Do those issues have anything to do with me?"

"Not at all. Of course, she wasn't happy to see you there, but our issues were way before that night."

"But I can't be helping the situation. How are you going to figure out what it is you're doing if I'm in the picture?"

"You said yourself, you don't want anything serious. When I asked you out, I knew in my heart it was wrong, but I honestly did want to get to know you. I'm not sure men in relationships should have new friends of the opposite sex, but I was intrigued, and it had nothing to do with me wanting to have sex with you. I admire the fuck out of your business, and it really was my intentions to pick your brain. Shit just went left. But I would never purposely hurt you. I don't want to hurt my baby moms either, and that's why I need to figure out what's good. If I choose to walk away from her, I know she'll be hurt, but I'm having a hard time trying to move past some shit right now."

I didn't like the fact that Biggs' death had numbed me the way that it did. The old Jayda would have been pissed that I was somehow a side chick. I would have cut Azaan off and never spoken to him again. I might have even been a little hurt, but the new Jayda wasn't. I was slightly disappointed that he was involved with someone, but that's life. After being single for four years, I'd suddenly come to the conclusion that maybe I would want to be in another relationship one day. Even that revelation took me by surprise. Before meeting Azaan, I was pretty much solidified on my stance that I'd never fall in love again. Now, just that fast, I was questioning it all.

"Until you figure out what it is that you need to figure out, maybe we should abstain from having sex," I suggested.

To my surprise, Azaan didn't look disappointed in the least. "Maybe you're right. I never want to be *that guy*. I'm not a creep. I'm not a bad guy, and I think you're dope as fuck. If friends is all we can be, then that's what it is."

Talk about having mixed feelings. I was lowkey upset that he didn't mind us not having sex again. His reaction to what I said really left me unsure about what I wanted, and I knew I needed to get my act together ASAP. I had managed to make it four years without getting myself caught up in any crazy situations. All I did was work and mind my business. I didn't need this fine ass man coming along and turning my world upside down because if he did decide to make things work with his baby mama, I didn't have time to be all sad and shit. He was a wonderful guy, but maybe he just wasn't on the market. After having a man of my own for five years that doted on me and loved me, I just couldn't see reducing myself to being a man's side chick. Even if the sex was phenomenal and he was absolutely gorgeous.

"How old is your son?" I decided to change the subject slightly. The way Azaan's eyes lit up when I asked about his son, it told me a lot about him.

"He's two." Like a proud parent, he pulled out his phone and showed me pictures.

My heart melted. "Oh my god, he's your twin."

"My little man is smart too. He can read two to three letter words, he can count, he's potty trained, and he knows some French."

I raised my eyebrows thoroughly impressed. "Wow. That is amazing."

Over lunch, we talked about how his club was coming along, and I told him that I enrolled back in school. He was damn near as excited as my dad, and that made me laugh. As he paid for our food, it hit me that I could spend all day with this man and not grow tired. I enjoyed his company just that much, so there you have it. It wasn't just the D that I liked. I actually liked Azaan as a person. Fuck. I wasn't sure what I was going to do about it, because even if I didn't reach out to him, Azaan never let too much time go by without reaching out to me. When he did reach out to me, I knew I wouldn't be strong enough to resist him, and that shocked me. I'd spent the last four years perfecting the art of being hard.

I was prepared to say a quick good-bye and retreat back to my place of business after Azaan walked me back to work, but he made even that difficult. Before I could even bid him farewell, Azaan had invaded my personal space and had placed the most sensual kiss on my lips. One that made my heart flutter.

"I hope you enjoy the rest of your day," he spoke as he peered into my eyes.

For just a few seconds, I was stuck. Stuck like hell, but I finally pulled myself together and found my voice. "What happened to all that we don't have to sleep together anymore, and if friends is all we'll ever be that's fine. Do friend kiss each other like that?" I inquired.

Azaan didn't respond with words. He kissed me hungrily and aggressively. My pussy ached for him as our tongues danced, and he kissed me like I was the long lost lover that he'd just found after searching for years. "I'd rather be your friend than nothing at all, but it's hard as hell acting like you don't do something to a nigga," he confessed with his forehead resting on mine. "You got a nigga's head fucked up. Bad." He placed one more succulent kiss on my lips before walking off.

I stared after him with a racing heart. If only he knew, he had my head fucked up too.

* * *

I WOKE up the next morning irritated beyond belief. I dreamed about Azaan the night before, and it really rubbed me the wrong way. This man was all of a sudden invading my thoughts, and I didn't like it. I don't care what kinds of problems they were having, technically, he belonged to somebody else. There wasn't anything I could do with that. Life had indeed gotten lonely and mundane, but I would never settle. I just couldn't. I thought about not going to work, but I decided against it. Work was one of the few things that I had to look forward to every day. I was for sure taking my ass to work.

When I got there and saw who was waiting for me, I almost wished I had stayed my ass home. Biggs' sister, Shonna was posted up in his Jag. We were cool as shit before he died, but after his mom basically put me out of his house after his death, I fed them with a long-handled spoon. I didn't make it a point to keep in touch, but when I saw them, I spoke. As I was heading for the door, Shonna got out of her car.

"Hi Jayda."

I stuck my key in the door and looked over my shoulder. "Hey, what's going on?" I was proud of the chipper voice that had managed to escape my lips.

"Have you talked to Romie?" she questioned, and that was odd to me. I hoped everything was okay with him. He'd been in the feds for three years with five more to go.

"Yes. I talked to him two days ago. Is everything okay?" I asked. My tone was laced with concern.

"I wrote him for Mommy two weeks ago, and he hasn't called her like I asked him to. The taxes are due on the house, and she needs help. She wanted to know if it would be okay for you to give her $400 out of Romie's cut of the business. After all, Biggs did start this business."

I had so much respect for Biggs that when his mother stated she wanted his house, I moved out with no questions asked. Biggs was a smart man, and he loved me. He may not have left me the house, but he made sure I was straight after he died. He could have left everything he had to his family, but he made sure I was straight, and that spoke volumes to me. It didn't matter that I wasn't his wife. He still wanted me to be good out here. I let his mother have the house that was paid for. She didn't have to pay a mortgage on it. All she had to do was pay the property taxes, and she couldn't even do that. I wasn't judging, and I wasn't trying to be mean, but she couldn't get shit out of me. Fuck her. Straight like that.

I put in the code for the alarm system. "Romie didn't mention it when we spoke, and I can't do anything with his cut of the money unless he asks me to. He normally calls me three times a week. Next time he calls, I'll ask him."

"A lien is going to be placed against the house if she doesn't pay the taxes, and they're already sixty days late. Can you just give her the money out of your cut? After all, this is Biggs' business."

She had the right one on the right day. That was the second time she'd mentioned it being Biggs' business as if I hadn't been the one working there and running it for the past four years. I didn't even attempt to hold back. "Maybe because I wasn't Biggs' wife, people think I wasn't shit to him, but Biggs loved me. He wanted to make sure I was straight, and he did that. He also knew he could trust me to keep his business afloat, and I've been doing that. I'm here six days a week. Romie also knows that I'm solid which is why he left me in charge. I didn't finish law school. I've been nursing this business since Biggs has been gone because it was *his* dream. I'm not rich. After I pay the store bills and give Romie his cut, I have just enough to live off of. Your mother wanted me out of the house, and I gave her that. She got all the furniture. I left there with nothing but my personal belongings. I even left her the food in the fridge. I'm not giving her anything else."

Shonna looked like she wanted to say something, but she didn't. She glared at me for a few seconds, and then she left. I didn't give a damn what Biggs' family thought of me. I tried to be as unproblematic as possible because I wasn't his wife, and we didn't have any kids together. All the shit they wanted like his house, his car, his jewelry, I let them have that. None of that mattered to me, but if his mom couldn't even pay the property taxes on the house, that wasn't my business. I wasn't giving her shit. Period.

5

## LIAH

Whn I opened my eyes, I saw that I was in a hospital room. I wasn't in any kind of pain, but I felt weak. I was also confused. My room was empty, and when I turned my head to the left and looked out of the window, I saw that sun was just beginning to set. What was I in the hospital for? I licked my dry lips and almost cut my tongue. That's how chapped my lips were. My throat was a little sore, and my mouth was extremely dry. As I looked around for the device so I could buzz a nurse, a flashback hit me, and the way that I gasped, you would have thought I got hit with a volt of electricity.

I just saw Dustin, getting in the car and telling me to drive. He was pale as fuck, and he looked terrified. Something with the robbery had gone wrong. The robbery. I did as Dustin asked, but before I could even make it off the street, he stopped talking. He was slumped over in the seat not moving, and I didn't know what to do. I then saw Azaan's face and a gun. He shot me. Tears flooded my eyes as I realized that I was alive. I was alive. Finding what I was looking for, I buzzed the nurse. I had no idea how long I'd been in the hospital. I was pretty sure that my friends were dead, and I didn't know why God favored me. Why was I the only one that made it? About a minute after I pressed the button, a nurse came into my room. She looked surprised when she saw that I was the only person in the room, and that I was awake. At that moment, I'd kill for something to drink. Every time I swallowed it felt like my throat was on fire. Swallowing was damn near painful. That's how dry my mouth was.

"Hi. You're awake," the nurse said as if me being awake was some sort of miracle.

"How long have I been here?" I croaked out. I barely had a voice.

"You were brought in two weeks ago with a gunshot wound to the left temple. After surgery, the doctor put you in a medically induced coma because there was swelling and bleeding in your brain. After a week, he took you off the medication that was inducing the coma. It took six days for you to wake up on your own."

"Can I have some water?" I asked in a hoarse voice as I processed the fact that I'd been in a coma for two weeks. Since the age of sixteen, not one day had passed without me being high. Now, I'd gone two weeks without snorting coke or popping any kind of pill. I hadn't even smoked any weed. It was a damn record. Maybe that's why despite feeling weak, I felt weird. Being sober wasn't something that I welcomed in the past. Being high was the norm for me.

"Sure dear. As soon as you drink this water, I'll get the doctor on duty so she can come speak with you."

I studied the nurse as she fixed me a drink. "Um, has anyone been here for me?" I was afraid of the answer, but it was a question that I had to ask.

She came over to my bed with the small paper cup full of water in hand. "Yes. Your parents come every day. For the first week, your mom and dad alternated spending the night with you. Your mom was here earlier, and so was your sister. They left about two hours ago."

At least that made my heart smile. Despite all that we'd been through and all the wrong I'd done, they came to see me every day. I drank the water down so fast that I almost choked and then instantly, my stomach began to rumble. The nurse looked down at me, her gaze filled with sympathy.

"Of course, when you came in we had to draw blood and run tests. You had an adequate amount of various drugs in your system. The good thing about you being out for two weeks is that you missed the bulk of the withdrawal symptoms, but I'm sure they aren't completely gone. All withdrawal symptoms are unpleasant, but they are a necessary evil. Your body is being rid of all that poison, and no matter how bad you might feel like you need the drugs, you don't."

I simply nodded. Before, I always got speeches on drugs when I was too high to give a fuck or when I was jonesin' for them and too sick to concentrate on what was being said. Now that I was sober, aside from probably pain medication, I really thought about what the nurse was saying to me. I hadn't been sober since I was a teenager. Everything that I did in my adult life was hard because of the fact that I loved doing drugs. I didn't have a car. I never really had my own place. I was homeless. Sleeping from couch to couch, roaming the streets all day with no real purpose other than getting high. There were plenty of days that I grew tired of living that way, and I wanted to go home. But the drugs had a hold over me. The life I lived wasn't my own. I was like a zombie. No matter how difficult drugs made life, it was still going to be hard not going back to them. Habits were a nasty thing to try and break and unfortunately, an addict had more triggers than anybody. A simple hard day at work could make you throw months of sobriety out of the window because you get so pissed that you pick up a crack pipe, or some coke, or some heroin.

My parents loved me, but I knew they didn't trust me. No way would my dad allow me to live in his home once I was released from the hospital, so where would I go? Dustin was dead and so was Sam. Tears blurred my vision as I thought about the fact that my two friends were dead all because it was my bright idea to rob Azaan. The nurse eased out of the room quietly, as I brought my hands up to my face and let out a good, long cry. How was I going to survive out in the world without the two people that knew me best and rocked with me with no judgement?

* * *

"Oh my god, Liah, you're up," my mother gasped when she walked into my hospital room several hours later carrying some magazines and a bag of food. She looked genuinely happy that I was up, and I suddenly felt like shit.

Shit for giving my parents hell when I was growing up when all they ever did was give me the best of everything. "Yeah, I woke up a few hours ago. The nurse helped me to take a shower, I brushed my teeth, and I ate. All of that wore me out, so I didn't even get around to my hair."

"I'll do it for you." My mom looked excited at the thought of doing my hair, and I smiled at her. It would take a lot of making up for me to get back in my parents' good graces. I had stolen from them, lied to them, and been all out disrespectful more times than I could ever count. "Would you like some food?" My mother dug through her bag. "I got a burger, some fries, and a milkshake."

"After two weeks of liquids, I think I need to ease into the solid food, but I am starving though. Two hours ago, I ate some soup, some Jell-O, and drank an Ensure. I'll take some of the milkshake if you don't mind." I felt shy and timid around my own mother, and I knew it was because of all the hell that I'd given her in the past. Feeling the guilt of it all while I was sober was a lot. Thinking about stealing my grams' ring from her made my face grow warm from embarrassment.

"Have you talked to the doctor?" she asked as she pulled a comb and brush from a bag that was on a table in the corner of my room. I hadn't even noticed it earlier.

"Yes. They ran a lot of tests and said they want to keep me for another few days for observation. Then I can go home." The word *home* came out in a much softer tone than the other words. I didn't have a home, and if I went back to the streets and old friends, I'd go back to drugs.

"Daddy is coming up here when he gets off work. I'm not sure he'll let you in the house to stay Liah, but I can give you money for a hotel room for a few nights. We can see how everything goes from there."

I nodded my head. I couldn't even be mad at that. I'd done a lot of wrong, and I knew it. I'd never be able to pay my parents back for all that I'd done to them. I lost count of how much money I stole from them. A twenty here, a ten there, a hundred dollars here, two hundred dollars there.

If I had to guess, I'd say I'd stolen more than ten thousand dollars from them, and I had absolutely nothing to show for it. Back when I was in high school, I'd steal enough money to buy an ounce of weed, and my friends and I would smoke it up in two or three days.

My mother and I sat in silence as she parted, combed, and braided my hair. "Have you talked to Jayda?" I finally asked.

"Yes. She called me yesterday while I was up here. She asks about you every day. She just enrolled back into law school."

"That's what's up." At least my parents had one child they could be proud of. I thought about what it would be like if I got myself together and got a job. I knew that if I put forth even an ounce of effort that my dad would dote on me and spoil me the same way he did Jayda. I could go from homeless and carless back to a life of luxury, and all I had to do was stay off drugs. I knew it wouldn't be easy, but I was honestly tired of not having shit and not being shit. Jayda lost her boyfriend, and she didn't even allow that to reduce her to the mess that I'd allowed myself to become. If she could kick life's ass so could I. People looked at me crazy all the time for having rich parents and pretty much choosing to not have shit. To be out here living in abandoned houses and sleeping in cars during the winter. I was finally tired. Maybe that bullet had slammed some sense into my brain.

My eyes widened when I thought about how I was at the trap that day and Azaan and Jayda seemed to know each other. He forbade his people from serving me because of some sort of allegiance to my sister. I wondered if she was really fucking with him like that and if so, how would she act if she found out that he was the one that shot me? Would she even care?

# 6

# JAYDA

"What you thinking about over there?" Azaan asked, breaking me from my thoughts.

I tore my eyes away from the pretty blue sky and looked over at his handsome chocolate face. It had been two days since I found out about his baby mama situation, and here I was with him yet again. We were on our way back from lunch. He was driving and taking me back to work.

I decided to be honest with him. "I'm wondering how I keep ending up with you. I mean, you say you're cool with us just being friends, but every time we hang out, the chemistry is undeniable. It hangs in the air like a thick fog. I feel it, and I know you do too. So how can we be *just* friends?"

Azaan glanced back at the road, and I knew he didn't have an immediate answer. His phone rang buying him some more time. "Hold that thought," he said as he picked his phone up out of the cup holder. "What's good?" Azaan listened to the caller for about a minute, and when he spoke, his voice was thick with irritation. "Say less. I'll be right there."

I looked over at him and saw that he was clenching his jaw muscles. He was obviously pissed about something. "Everything okay?"

He didn't respond right away. For a brief second, he continued to stare out at the road, but then he finally looked over at me. "Yeah, just some bullshit that I need to get a handle on. It'll only take me two minutes, and then I'll have you right back at work. I swear."

"It's fine. I'm the boss." I offered him a comforting smile. "I won't get in trouble if I'm late getting back."

He reached over and squeezed my hand, and it felt as if a million butterflies were fluttering around in my tummy. Azaan did something to me. No matter how hard I tried to fight it, the attraction was there. It didn't take me long to realize that we were heading into a seedy part of town. I didn't become too alarmed, but when Azaan pulled up in front of a run-down looking house with three men in the front yard, two of them clearly arguing with an older man that appeared to be on drugs, my breath caught in my throat. Azaan reached under his seat, and I jerked my head over in his direction. My heart rate increased as I saw a shiny chrome gun in his hand. He threw his car door open and jumped out of the car. He stormed over to the men, and I could feel my heart beating in my throat.

Azaan left his car door open, so I could hear everything that was being said. "What I'm saying to you is my girlfriend sold my pain pills without my permission, and I need them back. I take those pills because my back is messed up, and she didn't have a right to give them to you in exchange for whatever you gave her," he yelled.

"And muhfucka I told you—" a tall man began to shout, but Azaan cut him off.

"Get the fuck from in front of my spot right got damn now. I don't know what you got going on, but you need to take that shit up with ya bitch. You been out here entirely too long causing a scene, and that shit ends now. You gon' fuck around and be leaving this bitch in a body bag, and then you won't need no pain pills," Azaan growled.

My hands started to tremble and a light blanket of sweat decorated my nose. My eyes were fixated on the shiny gun in Azaan's hand. It was taking me back to a place that I didn't want to ever revisit.

"Nigga—"

That was all the man could get out of his mouth before Azaan raised his arm and brought the butt of the gun crashing into his mouth. As if on cue, the other two men started beating the man, and it didn't take any time for his body to hit the ground. From there they proceeded to stomp him out. I couldn't take it anymore. I opened the car door and took off walking. I had no idea where I was going, but I couldn't stay there. It took me a moment to realize that Azaan was calling my name and another second for me to realize that I was hyperventilating.

"Jayda!" He was right behind me.

I whirled around with tears in my eyes. "Why the fuck would you bring me—" I couldn't even get the rest of the words out. My chest heaved up and down, and I struggled to breathe. All I saw was me holding Biggs in my arms and him taking his last breath.

When Azaan saw the state that I was in, he immediately looked regretful. He attempted to grab me, but I jerked away from him. "Leave me the fuck alone," I growled through clenched teeth. "Why the fuck would you even —" Again, I couldn't finish talking. I stood still and tried to steady my breathing.

Azaan wrapped his arm around my waist, and I struggled to get away from him, but he only held me tighter. "I'm sorry Jayda. I would never put you in danger. I swear I wouldn't. That was a little bullshit situation, but I would never. I'm sorry. I forgot what you went through."

His tone was calm and reassuring. I steadied my breathing and wiped my tears. "Can you take me back to my job?" He was still holding onto me tight.

"Not until I know you're good. Look at me."

I hesitated to do as he asked. I would never feel ashamed for the fact that I was traumatized. Maybe to some I was overreacting, but if you've never watched your soulmate take his last breath over some dumb shit, then you could never. I wouldn't ever completely be okay again and dumb ass arguments and street beef were my triggers. How could Azaan be so sure that man wouldn't leave, go get a gun, and come back. Yes, the entire scene took me back to the day of Biggs' murder, but it also made me realize something else. I really liked Azaan, and if something happened to him, I'd be crushed. It wouldn't hurt me as badly as losing Biggs did, but it would hurt.

"Jayda, I'm sorry. Look at me, please," he was pleading.

Losing Biggs taught me that life was short. Fronting, acting hard, all that shit meant nothing at the end of the day. Time was too short to be anything other than real. I turned to look at him, and when I spoke, I spoke with conviction. "I've allowed myself to get caught up in some bullshit. I like you way too much. You belong to somebody else, and here I am spending damn near all my free time with you and feeling things for you. Why would you even put me through that? If something happened to you, how do you think that would make me feel? What are we even doing Azaan?"

"I'm not going anywhere Jayda." He peered into my eyes. That statement gave me no comfort. It wasn't an answer, but I didn't press the issue. He placed a soft kiss on my lips. "You heard me?"

"I heard you."

"You want to go back to work or you want to go home?"

"I'm going back to work."

I walked back to the car and Azaan got in. I didn't know where his homies or the man they beat went, but none of the them were in the front yard any longer. We were almost fifteen minutes away from my job, and we rode there in silence. A million thoughts were running through my mind. When Azaan finally pulled up at my job, I took my seat belt off.

"Jayda."

I looked over at Azaan, and he truly looked sorry. "It's okay."

"Come here."

I leaned over the arm rest, and he sat up. Placing his lips on mine, Azaan snaked his tongue into my mouth. He kissed me with enough passion to have my pussy throbbing. He broke the kiss and moved his lips over to my neck and French kissed it. A slight moan escaped my lips. Azaan finally stopped the assault on my flesh and peered into my eyes. "Enjoy the rest of your day. I'll call you later."

Tired of resisting my feelings for him, I placed a kiss on his lips before emerging from the car. Fuck it. I already knew God wasn't playing fair when he took Biggs from me. Maybe what I was starting with Azaan was forbidden and unconventional because he wasn't really single, but I didn't give a damn. There was no black and white, cut and dry with life. There were a whole bunch of gray areas and sometimes, you just have to go with the got damn flow.

# 7

# VICKIE

The deadline for me to have Meer's money had come and gone, and I hadn't heard from him. It had been more than three days, and I was actually getting happy. Maybe he'd changed his mind about blackmailing me. Maybe the nigga had jumped off a bridge. I really didn't care. I just wanted him to leave me alone. With him suddenly going MIA, my thoughts were back on fixing my relationship with Azaan. He hadn't given me a date on when he was coming back to Miami to visit, and since I wanted him to avoid running into Meer, I decided to take Aheem to visit him. No way would he make me leave early or turn me away if I popped up with his son on my hip. No bitch on the face of this Earth would ever make Azaan front on his son, I didn't care how mad he was with me. No way was I driving for seven hours with a two-year-old, so I booked us flights. I knew what Azaan said about him not wanting us to live there with him, but we were going to visit for a good two weeks. No way was I going to sit back and let another bitch spend more time with my man than me. I would beg him every day to forgive me if I had to.

Plus, if I was in North Carolina, I could avoid Meer's bitch ass too. It wasn't my fault he didn't come get the money when he was supposed to. All of my good, positive, happy thoughts went out the window when I got back home from taking Aheem to daycare, and Meer's hoe ass was parked in my driveway. He was leaning up against a white Camry that probably belonged to his mother or some female that he was screwing. I knew it wasn't his. My upper lip curled into a snarl as I slammed my car door shut and walked over to him. I absolutely loathed his ass. Meer looked at me with a smirk on his face.

"How's it going Love? I know I'm a few days late. See, I'm a reasonable guy, and I wanted to give you every opportunity to have my money. All of it. I didn't want there to be any excuses. Looking around this huge ass house, this big ass yard, these luxury cars, I should have asked for more."

I had taken everything out of my bank account except for $1,000. There was no way I was emptying my bank account for this fuck nigga, and I refused to give him a dime of Azaan's money. Seeing as how Azaan already knew about us, I shouldn't be giving him anything, but I just wanted him out of my hair. I never wanted to see Meer's face again. I hated to burst his bubble, but it had to be done. "Well it isn't everything you asked for," I snapped. "I gave you what I had. Azaan's money is his, and I'm not giving you one dime of his money. Fuck you," I spat boldly. "Now you can take what I have, or I can call Azaan to handle your ass. The choice is yours."

Meer whipped a gun from the waistband of his basketball shorts. I instantly got the cotton mouth, and my eyes darted around me to see if any of my neighbors were outside. Hell no. "I'm tired of playing with you. That shit is a muhfuckin' rap," he sneered. "Get in the fuckin' house and run me that bag."

I walked towards my front door. There was nothing stopping him from robbing Azaan. Being that my mom had her own business that I worked at sometimes, I had two bank accounts. One with my own money in it and one with Azaan's money in it. After his mom passed, he also got the money from her policy, flipped it, and took a large amount and opened a bank account. He took the paperwork from the policy to prove that he was the beneficiary. No one questioned as to why he cashed the check at one place and put the cash in another. The bank was just happy to get the business. That was a good way for him to wash his money, and every year he adds more to it.

With the two bank accounts he already had, plus the business account for the club, there was no need for Azaan to keep super large amounts of money in the house. Last time I counted, the safe in the closet had a little over $40,000 but that wasn't all of his money by far. We had that at our disposal for emergencies. That amount of money was a drop in the bucket for Azaan, but he'd no doubt be pissed if Meer got his hands on it.

Once I unlocked the front door, Meer shoved me inside. "To your bedroom," he growled, and I knew he was going for the safe.

I led him through the house to the bedroom that I shared with Azaan. Our décor was gray and silver. The bed was made, I had a candle burning so it smelled like vanilla in there, and everything was neat and clean. After a long day, I loved curling up in my bed and enjoying the lavish surroundings that Azaan's hard work afforded me. I could tell that Meer had never been in anything as nice and that he was impressed.

"Tuh, y'all muhfuckas doing it real big huh?" he marveled in a voice laced with envy. I didn't respond. He pushed me down on the bed. "Before I get my money, let me get some pussy for the road." A devilish grin slid across his face.

My heart pounded like an African drum. "Meer, please. No," I begged as I backed up towards the headboard. I didn't give a damn about my shoes being on my $300 comforter.

He walked around the bed, came over to me, and slapped the shit out of me. My cheek stung so badly that it brought tears to my eyes. "You still telling me no when it should be obvious that I'm not playing with your bitch ass. You gon' suck this muhfuckin' dick or you gon' suck the barrel of my gun," he barked as he pulled his ashy dick out.

A salty tear ran into my mouth as I slid my hands behind the pillow that was beside me. While Meer was taking off his shorts and boxers, I pulled my .22 from its confinement and shot his pussy ass in the midsection before he could even blink. With wide eyes and a startled expression on his face, Meer clutched his stomach and fell back into the dresser. Azaan demanded that a gun be kept in every room of the house because of the life he lived. Even with a top of the line home security system, he still had more than five guns stashed throughout the house, so needless to say, we had to be very careful with a toddler in the house.

"Bitch," Meer yelled out through clenched teeth as he slid down the dresser onto the floor. My crème carpeted floor. The carpet would for sure have to be ripped up.

With my trembling hands still holding the gun, I stared down at his body. He was still alive and bleeding on my carpet, but he wouldn't be for long.

# 8

## AZAAN

"**Y**ou fucking with me?" I asked Jayda as I stared into her eyes and grinded into her. It was my first time ever sexing her without a condom, and that shit felt like heaven. Her soft hand was caressing my cheek as I moved in and out of her slowly. I wanted to hear the words fall off her lips. That shit would do something to a nigga's ego.

"I'm fucking with you," she whispered softly. She was barely done talking before I covered my lips with hers and we engaged in a passionate kiss. Shorty had my head fucked up, and I wasn't afraid to admit it.

I wasn't sure what it was. Maybe it was the way she was guarded and determined not to let me in. Initially, I thought fucking with her would be perfect because she wasn't trying to get attached, but now we both were. Attached. I wasn't fucking with Vickie at the moment, but she was still very much in my life. I wasn't sure why I was setting myself up for some bullshit, but I was diving into the fire head first.

Jayda wrapped her legs around my waist and started winding her hips in a circular motion. "I'm about to cum," she declared in a low tone, eyes closed, hand still caressing my cheek. She bit her bottom lip, and I gently bit her neck.

"Vous vous sentez bien," I whispered in her ear in French, telling her that she felt good. Whenever I spoke French it was a hit with the ladies, and Jayda was no exception to the rule. She moaned seductively, and the grip her pussy had on my dick tightened. "Cum on this dick," I demanded in a low voice as I kept my same rhythm.

"Fuuckkkk," she whimpered as her pussy muscles contracted on my dick.

"Ummmmmmm," I grunted. I couldn't help it. The grip her vagina had on my dick pulled the seeds out of me, and they spilled right into her. I hoped she wouldn't be pissed, but no way could I pull out. Not while she was cumming too. I pulled out of her and rolled onto my back so I could catch my breath.

Turmoil had never felt so good. I knew the deeper that I got in with Jayda, the more problems it would bring me but instead of running away from the problems, I seemed to be running towards them. I snapped out of my thoughts when Jayda entered the room with a warm rag and proceeded to clean me off like she always did. I studied her intently, admiring her strikingly beautiful features. It was a wonderful thing when a woman had the personality to go along with her beauty. Even with her baggage and all that she'd been through, Jayda had pulled me in, and I didn't want her to let me go.

My phone rang, and I grabbed it up off her nightstand. Seeing that it was Vickie, I didn't hesitate to answer. A lot of the times that she called me these days it wasn't about my son. It was about her wanting us to work on us, but I still answered whenever she called because I never knew when it was about my son. "Hello?" I answered, sitting up.

"Azaan, I need you," Vickie sniffed, and I could tell that she was crying. At first, I thought she was just being dramatic until she kept talking. "Something happened. At the house. I need you here *now*."

Vickie knew better than to talk over the phone so her being vague didn't take away from me knowing that something was wrong. The strain in her voice was obvious and when she said something happened at the house, I was immediately alarmed. I sat up. "You good? Where is Aheem?"

"He's at daycare. I asked my mom to pick him up. Azaan, I need you to fly. Driving will take too long." It was urgent. Had niggas broken in and did they have her held hostage or some shit?

"You didn't answer my question. Are you good? Are you at the house alone?"

"Yeah. I am." Her voice was low. Vickie didn't sound right.

"I'm on my way."

I hopped up and began getting dressed with a million thoughts running through my mind. Home invasion, the police, what could it be? Jayda took the cloth she had in the bathroom then came back out as I sat down on the edge of her bed trying to find a flight home.

"Is everything okay?"

"I'm not sure," I answered truthfully never taking my eyes off the phone. "Fuuuckkk." I didn't see anything leaving before the next four hours, and it was frustrating. Shit, with a four-hour head start, I'd be halfway home by the time the plane landed but even with having to wait for a flight, flying was faster than driving. I was still contemplating taking my chances, but instead I just booked the flight. I needed to get home, take a shower, and hit the road. I had a whole house in Miami, so I didn't need luggage.

I finally stood up and looked at Jayda. "I have to catch a flight to Miami. I'm not sure when I'll be back, but I'll hit you up."

"Okay."

I leaned in and brushed my lips across hers. For as much fun as I was having with Jayda and for as much as I liked her, my home came first.

* * *

I HOPPED out of the Uber with sweaty palms. I hadn't spoken to Vickie since she called me hours before. I knew she couldn't talk over the phone, and I wasn't interested in trying to decipher riddles, so I just decided to wait. Finally, I was home. Her cars were parked in the driveway and so were mine. One thing stood out to me, and I immediately became alarmed. A white Camry that I'd never seen before was parked in my driveway. I wasn't really sure what to expect, but I couldn't get a gun through the airport, so I prayed to God that I wasn't about to walk into some sort of ambush. If niggas had Vickie at gunpoint or some shit then I was walking into a deadly situation naked. Using my key, I entered the house, and I found Vickie sitting on the couch with a tear streaked face smoking a blunt. When she saw me, she hopped up off the couch and ran into my arms. She buried her face into my chest and cried. I was relieved to see that she appeared to be in the house alone.

"Vickie what's good? What happened?" I inquired in a soothing tone.

Instead of speaking, she pulled her face from my shirt and grabbed my hand. She led me through the house to our bedroom. My face crumpled with irritation because if what she'd done was a ploy to get me home to talk to her, then she was about to see a side of me that she'd never seen before, and I meant that shit with everything in me. I was just about to snatch my hand out of hers and ask her what was good, when we neared the bedroom and a putrid smell invaded my nostrils and made me gag.

"What the fuck?" I asked, covering my nose with my shirt. The smell was foul as fuck.

Vickie pulled me into the bedroom, and my eyes damn near popped out of the sockets. "What the fuck?" I asked, stunned as I saw Meer laid out on my bedroom floor, eyes open, dead as fuck. My carpet was stained with his maroon-colored blood and his body had released his bowels. The sight was gory, and the smell was stomach turning. "Vickie what the fuck?" I asked, looking at a mess that I obviously had to clean up.

"That muhfucka came in here demanding twenty-five thousand dollars from me to leave town. I was going to give him seventeen, but that's all I had. He said he didn't want short money, and he was about to rape me. I pulled the gun from behind the pillows, and I killed him. I didn't call the police because how would we explain to your aunt that I shot her son for trying to rape me? His cousin's girl."

I had to leave the room. I'd seen plenty of dead bodies, but even holding my nose and breathing through my mouth, it's like I could still smell the shit. I walked in the living room so pissed that I was surprised I wasn't breathing fire. Vickie was right behind me. "Why the fuck was he in my house? He didn't just come today asking for that money. How many times have you seen him? When did he get out?" I asked her with fire blazing in my eyes. I wasn't a perfect nigga by far, but it was too much fuck shit going on with Vickie and my cousin for my liking. Shit wasn't adding up.

Vickie took a step back. A clear indication that she was nervous. I didn't give a damn about her being nervous. There was a dead body in my bedroom. In my home where I lay my head, where my son laid his head. I was also going to have to involve other people because Vickie was right about one thing. There was no way to explain to my aunt how her son ended up dead in my crib. I mean I could but, I loved my aunt too much to let her know that her son was a sleaze ball ass nigga that was basically extorting my girl. I'd have to get my most trusted hittas to help me clean this mess up. Meer's body had to be disposed of, and the carpet would have to be pulled up from my bedroom floor and destroyed. I wasn't expecting to walk into my home to this shit.

"H-he showed up here a few days ago. He said that he wanted money to leave town or else he was going to be a problem for you. I know I should have told you, but I just wanted him to go away. I wanted him out of our hair. I emptied my bank account for him. I refused to give him one dime of your money, so everything I was going to give him was mine." Tears streamed down Vickie's face as she explained herself to me.

My blood began to boil with rage. "Do I look like that muhfucka puts fear in my heart?" I roared, causing her to jump slightly. "This nigga said he was gon' be a problem for me?" I balled my face up in disdain. "This nigga had the nerve to show up on my doorstep and instead of letting me know, you was gon' give money to the fuck nigga? Fuck is wrong with you?" I asked through clenched teeth. I was ready to put my fists through something. Either a wall or Vickie's face.

"I know that you weren't threatened by Meer. He was just talking crazy saying that you aren't superhuman and that if he catches you slipping it could end bad for you. I just didn't want him coming for you Azaan."

"So why not give me a heads up?! You think keeping me in the dark was beneficial to me? You're supposed to be the first one to let me know if a nigga got plans to come at me. You think that nigga was gon' take that bread and get ghost? You never been that green baby. Be for real. I'm disappointed Vickie. You moved sneaky and suspect as fuck concerning Meer. But I'm supposed to look at you and trust you?" I asked with my upper lip curled into a snarl.

"Yes, you are," she cried with conviction. "I may have gone about it the wrong way, but I got your back. I always have."

"I can't tell."

I turned my back on her and called my man Snootie. He was Mexican and had been in the country for three years. His English wasn't good at all, but the nigga knew how to get money. He copped pills from me heavy and slung them in his hood. Snootie be putting in work, and he solid as fuck. I knew I could call him and one other person, and they'd get rid of Meer for a fee, of course. Snootie was an immigrant that broke the law several times a day. I for damn sure wasn't worried about him snitching and for the right amount of cash, I knew he'd do a thorough job. Thanks to my rules, Meer wasn't able to get one up on Vickie. If I didn't make it mandatory for there to be a gun in every room in my home, she might be the dead body lying on the floor instead of him.

Even if the body was disposed of and the carpet replaced, I didn't want my son sleeping in a house or being in a room where a muhfucka was bodied. There wasn't enough sage in the world to make me okay with that shit, so now I had to deal with the task of moving. All of this shit was Vickie's fault in my eyes.

Vickie waited for me to get off the phone with Snootie before she spoke again. "Is Meer really the reason that you're mad at me now or is it that bitch in North Carolina?"

I took a deep breath to keep from saying something really disrespectful. "I just had to call my mans to come get a dead body off my fuckin' floor," I seethed. "The shit is going to have to be disposed of, meaning my aunt will never know what happened to her son. I gotta live with that shit.

Every time I see her, I'm gon' have to front like I don't know shit. Look that woman in the eyes and act like I don't know that her only son is worm food. Then, I gotta make sure you and my son have somewhere to stay. Don't talk to me about no fuckin' female right now." I glared at her.

"Not talking about her isn't going to bring Meer back. I need to know what's good with you and her. Matter of fact, why can't Aheem and I just come to North Carolina with you for a while? He misses you."

I took a step towards her. "What the fuck did I say? Until I get all of this shit cleared up don't talk to me about shit." I stormed past her and headed outside to wait for Snootie. How in the hell could I answer questions about Jayda when I wasn't even sure what was going on my damn self?

# 9

# DIOR

"What's good? Everything straight with us?" Marshon asked after the camera crew left and we'd wrapped for the night. It was the night that I popped up on him at his show out of town to "fix" our relationship issues.

I licked my lips nervously. "Yeah. I just, I kind of feel bad about that night. I mean, you're handsome, and you're a cool guy, but I wasn't thinking clearly. That pill had me fucked up. I'm in a relationship."

Marshon let out a light chuckle. "Aye, I swear I commend you for wanting to keep it real with your dude. I know females that were fucking the same day their man got knocked, so it's nice to know there are still some stand-up women left, but he's prison, and he has been for over a year. You can't feel bad because for one night you put your feelings first. The way you was bustin' on my dick, you needed that release shawty," Marshon stated with a lustful gleam in his eyes.

My face flushed with embarrassment. I didn't care what he or Nico said. Yeah, maybe if the tables were turned and it was me locked up, Fahan would have been sleeping with other women, but I still felt guilty. Especially now that we were getting married. I just wanted to put that night with Marshon behind me, and that was hard to do with him licking those pink ass, pussy sucking lips. Memories of our night together flashed through my mental, and a chill started at the base of my spine and crept up to my neck.

"Yeah, I guess I did," I stated in a low voice. "Anyway, I'm about to head out. It's only a two-hour drive home, so I'll see you next time we film." Nico was waiting for me at the hotel bar.

"You sure you want to drive home? You can stay with me. I'm here until tomorrow."

I contemplated it for a brief, and I do mean a very brief, second. I couldn't even shake the guilt from the first time so there was no way I was doing it again. Fahan now had a little more than four months before he came home, and I could wait four months. The worst thing I could do was make cheating on him a habit.

"No, I got my friend with me, but thanks for the offer though." I shot Marshon a friendly smile and left his room quick, fast and in a hurry.

As soon as I stepped onto the elevator, it's like my pussy began to ache for Marshon. It's like it was sending a signal to my brain to run back into that hotel room and get dicked down real proper. I was depriving myself for love. If Fahan came home and cheated on me, I'd gut his ass like a fish. Being out here in the real world passing up dick was a hard ass feat. Especially when the dick you were passing up was good and about to be rich as fuck. Once the elevator doors slid open, I stepped off and headed for the bar. Out of nowhere I was horny as shit, and I knew it was because I was in the same building as Marshon. I spotted Nico at the bar and walked over to him. "You ready?"

It had been an eventful day of filming. His dramatic ass was made for the camera, and the producers loved him. They'd already asked him to come back and shoot with me, and he ate that shit up. As soon as Nico looked at me, I could tell he was drunk as a skunk. "Yes ma'am, I am ready. Did you slob all on your boo?" Nico flicked his tongue in and out of his mouth provocatively, causing me to roll my eyes upwards.

"Bring your drunk ass on. I don't have time to play with you. Marshon is not my boo, and I'm never slobbing on him again." I turned on my heels and headed for the door.

Nico followed me. "Girl, you sure are crazy. He all muscular and fine and tatted up and about to be rich, and you're passing up on that dick for a nigga in pri-son," Nico said the word *prison* all dramatic like.

I whirled around to face him causing him to stop walking abruptly. "I want everybody to stop reminding me that my nigga is in prison. I know very well where he is. If I want to keep my vagina to myself while I wait on him to come home, that's my business. Fahan is fine, muscular, tatted up, and he for sure isn't going to be broke once he starts working at the club, so let me worry about mine," I hissed.

Nico threw his hands up in surrender. His lowcut hair was dyed blue, and he was dressed in tight denim True Religion jeans and a matching blue shirt that was a tad bit too small and hugged his little belly. His nails were short and painted with clear nail polish, his lips were coated with clear gloss, and his thick eyebrows were arched to perfection. Nico dressed like the man that he was, but he was almost more feminine than me.

"You don't have to read me for filth boo. If you don't want a fine ass man to knock the dust off that cat, that's your business, but let's go. Your grumpy ass can get me back to Charlotte expeditiously because I do have a dick appointment."

I turned and headed for my car. I was in a bad mood because everyone kept acting like I was wrong for holding Fahan down. It's not like he got sentenced to ten years. Less than two years wasn't a lot when you really loved someone. I slipped up once, but that didn't mean I had to keep doing it. If I was being honest with myself, I'd have to acknowledge that I was also grumpy because at that moment, all I really wanted to be doing was riding Marshon's dick.

* * *

I WOKE up the next day in a much better mood. After I got done with filming I was going to take some of the money that Azaan gave me and go and purchase a simple wedding band for Fahan. I couldn't believe that we were getting married. All of the lonely nights and hard days without him would be worth it. From the day he stepped foot out of prison, he was going to be part owner of a legit business. We were already making plans to move into a nice house once the lease on the apartment was up. He told me that I could sell all my furniture when we moved, and get new stuff. I was going to be somebody's wife. Not just anybody's wife, a successful ass man. He also told me he wanted us to honeymoon in Haiti so I could get to know his family. I had a lot of planning to do and a lot to look forward to, and I wasn't going to let Marshon's dick knock me off my square. We were filming at one of the pregnant girl's gender reveal. She was the one on the show whose man had a side chick and they got into a fight at the mall. Her name was Sky, and she was my favorite person out of all the girls. She did a good job on camera of acting like she wasn't pressed about the side chick Sahara and acting all tough, but I'd heard her crying on the phone to her dude when the cameras weren't rolling. Their storyline wasn't fake, and I felt bad for her because she was a sweet girl.

I just didn't see how anyone could put all their hurtful personal business out for the world to see all for a check. I was ear hustling and heard her say that she's getting $5,000 per episode and that made sense because her man was already established, but fuck all that. I wouldn't let the world know that my man was playing the heck out of me. Not even for five stacks per episode. I dressed in an all-white romper with some gold heels. Since there was a make-up artist on set, I left my face bare. I elected to go with my black wet-n-wavy hair that hung down to my ass. I was sure that Sky would have liquor at the event because we rarely ever filmed without drinking. Despite that fact, I still went into my kitchen and poured myself a shot of tequila to calm my nerves. A few times it was mad early or we did scenes at the gym, so we didn't drink alcohol, but liquor and wine calmed our nerves and relaxed us. It was hard getting used to having cameras in your face. The producers didn't hesitate to feed us alcohol either because most of the girls got turned up when they're drinking and that meant more drama.

I just looked at the producers and shook my head sometimes. Yeah, they're paying us so they wanted the show to be good and have high ratings, but all they cared about was drama. They hyped shit up so there's an argument or a fight pretty much every day. So far, I'd managed to do a good job of staying out of the bullshit. I didn't want to come across as too boring because then they might not invite me back for season two, but I was going to keep what Fahan said in the back of my mind. I wasn't going to sell my soul for a dollar.

Two shots of tequila gave me the warm buzz that I needed. I hopped in my car and headed to the location so I could get my day started. I wanted to get home at a decent time and be well rested for my visit the next day with Fahan. Seeing him always excited me and made me feel like a giddy school girl with a crush. I pulled up at the location and headed inside to get my make-up done. The make-up artist Gia started right away, and she made small talk as she did my make-up. She'd been working on me for about ten minutes, when out of nowhere I was hit with a 'bout of nausea that almost made me double over. I gripped the sides of the chair that I was sitting in as if I was bracing myself for something. My chest heaved up and down, and Gia immediately stopped what she was doing and took a step back. "Are you okay?" she asked with concern.

I hiccupped. A clear sign that I was about to puke. Pulling myself up out of the chair, I rushed to the bathroom down the hall and made it just in time to puke up my guts in the trash can by the door. I held tightly onto the sides of the trash can as I dry heaved. All I had to eat that day was some eggs and grits and then I had the two shots of tequila. I was so busy throwing up the contents of my stomach that I didn't realize Kylie, one of the producers, had come into the bathroom until I heard water running and I saw her through my peripheral vision as spit hung off my bottom lip. She wet some paper towels and handed them to me.

"Thank you," I stated as tears ran down my cheeks. I had thrown up so hard that it brought tears to my eyes.

"Are you okay?"

I wiped my mouth. "Um yeah, I guess. I don't know. I just feel sick all of a sudden. I should be able to get through at least a few hours of filming. Maybe I ate something bad last night." I struggled to remember everything I'd eaten the day before as I headed over to the sink to rinse my mouth out. "You think there's an extra toothbrush somewhere or does anyone at least have some mouthwash?" I frowned up at the awful taste in my mouth.

"I can run to the store and grab you a toothbrush. Do I need to get a pregnancy test while I'm at it?"

My head snapped in her direction so fast that shit hurt my neck. I ignored the pain as my eyebrows furrowed from confusion. "Why in the hell would you need to get me a pregnancy test?"

Kylie shrugged her shoulder with a dumbfounded look on her face. Me and the girls often joked that she looked like Kylie Jenner before the surgery. Her ass had no lips, no ass, no nothing. Her skin was super pale. She dressed like she just didn't care about life, but she for sure wasn't broke, because she drove a yellow Porsche. "Are you on birth control? Do you and Marshon use protection? I mean, even if you do, the viewers won't know that. We could use the possibility of you being pregnant as a story line. We can stretch it for at least two episodes."

Kylie looked all happy and giddy, meanwhile my stomach felt like it plummeted to my feet. I wanted to snap on her. Tell her that my sex life was none of her business, but I did have unprotected sex with Marshon, and he came in me. Several times. The horror of it all knocked me into the wall behind me. I stood there with a dumbfounded expression on my face while my heart raced a mile a minute. I wanted to cry, but I was paralyzed from fear. I couldn't move. I could barely breathe, and Kylie was just staring at me soaking all that shit up.

"I'll go get you a test."

I knew that shooting wasn't going to stop for me. I knew I needed to go back inside the dressing room and continue getting my make-up done, but I just couldn't move. I stared off into space for what felt like an eternity as I thought about just how stupid I'd been. Taking that ecstasy pill had led to a string of bad decisions that I was regretting more and more each day. And in a world where plan B pills were plentiful, how could I have been so stupid? I was too mad at myself to even cry. Finally, I peeled myself off the wall and headed back inside to get my make-up done. I wanted so hard to pretend that everything was okay, but I was so scared that my hands were trembling. I said a silent prayer and begged God to just get me out of this mess. If I was pregnant there was no doubt about the fact that I was getting an abortion. There was no other possible outcome, but I didn't even want to have to go through any of that. I didn't want to be pregnant with another man's baby for an hour, a day, or a week. I had learned my lesson the hard way, and I'd been scared straight. I swear.

"You good boo?" Gia still wore a look of concern on her face.

I nodded and sat down in the chair. "Yeah. I think I must have eaten something bad," I said in a small voice and offered a weak smile.

"Girl, you look pale as shit," Gia observed.

When I sat down and observed my reflection in the mirror, I did look ghastly. I sat there, mind racing as she tried to hurry up and finish my make-up. I made an effort to steady my breathing and act as normal as possible, but a bitch was about to piss on herself. I had never been pregnant before in my life, and I honestly thought that my first pregnancy would be by Fahan. After he'd been home for a while and the club was doing good. I knew that my fifteen minutes of fame could only last so long, even if I did get asked to be back on the reality show for a second season. I was going to get as much accomplished as I possibly could. When Azaan gave me more money, I paid my bills and still had almost two thousand dollars left over. I spent five hundred of that adding more inventory to my boutique. I wasn't going to actually start promoting the website until after the show started airing on TV. Hopefully, my social media followers would go out and they would buy out my inventory.

Aside from the boutique, I decided that I might try my hand at selling bundles. Once I became popular, I could pretty much sell anything and people would buy it. I spent a lot of nights brainstorming. After I had a few successful businesses under my belt, I'd love nothing more than to carry Fahan's child. Me having a child by anyone else was utterly unacceptable. About fifteen minutes passed before Kylie stuck her head in the door and signaled for me to come to her.

"Almost done," Gia stated as she rubbed some gloss on my lips.

I literally felt like I was going to pass out. I was lightheaded and the way my stomach was churning, I was scared that I was going to throw up again. Once Gia was done, she moved out of the way so I could look in the mirror. All I could do was offer another fake, weak smile.

"Thank you. It's very pretty."

"Feel better girl. I can tell you don't feel good." Gia looked at me pitifully.

I stood up on wobbly knees and headed for the door. I wasn't even sure why I was allowing Kylie to even be this far up in my business. My mind was clouded, I was terrified, and I wasn't thinking clearly. At all. I followed her into the bathroom, and she pulled a pregnancy test from the bag. No words were spoken as she handed it to me, and I eased inside a stall and closed the door. No lie, it took me almost five minutes to get the test open. That's how nervous I was. Finally, I got it open, and I peed on the stick. I couldn't recall having ever been so nervous in my entire life. All I could think of was if I got out of this shit, I would never, ever cheat again.

I beat myself up mentally for so long that I lost track of time. By the time I looked down at the test in my hand, there were two pink lines as clear as day staring back up at me, and I bawled like a baby.

"Dior, what is it? Let me in." It was Kylie.

I knew that she would want to put this bullshit on the show. My life was falling apart, and she was worried about her fuck ass show, but I had already assured Fahan that my entire storyline was fake. If the producers made me tell Marshon on camera that I was pregnant, I'd say it was a lie. By the time Fahan came home, I would have gotten an abortion and put all this shit behind me. Kylie knocked lightly on the door and used the back of my hand to wipe my tears away before opening the door.

"It's positive?" she questioned with what appeared to be concern on her face. I couldn't be for sure if she really cared about how I felt or if she just wanted me to think that she did. Either way, I didn't care. As soon as I got a chance, I was calling to schedule an abortion. Nothing on the face of the Earth could make me have Marshon's baby.

"Yeah it is, but it's fine. Listen, I know I agreed to be on the show but let me tell Marshon in my own way." I knew there was no need for me to tell her not to tell him. All the producers on the show cared about were entertaining, drama-filled scenes. I'd have an easier time convincing Fahan that I wasn't pregnant than to convince Kylie to leave this shit completely out of the show.

"Of course Dior but remember, if this show does well and gets good ratings, within days of the show airing, you can be in a completely different tax bracket. The more your storyline brings to the show, the more money you'll be able to ask for next season. Five thousand dollars an episode times at least twelve episodes means a lot of money in your bank account."

Like I predicted. All she cared about was episodes and money, but she was right. If I could be on the show for as many seasons as I could, my bank account would be sitting lovely. It was my hopes that even if my storyline with Marshon ended, they'd keep me around. Once Fahan came home, I wasn't even sure he'd let me keep being on the show, but I'd worry about all of that later. I tossed the pregnancy test in the trash can and washed my hands. Then I exited the bathroom without saying anything.

* * *

"WHAT'S UP? The producers told me to come check on you. You good?" Marshon asked me after the gender reveal scene was over.

I was walking out to my car and I looked up and saw cameras behind him. "Get that camera the fuck out of my face," I hissed at Mark, the camera guy. "I knew Kylie was going to run her fucking mouth. You're going to get your precious drama, but you're not getting it until I get ready to give it to you," I spat before walking off.

Marshon had a confused expression on his face. "Dior hold up, what's going on?"

I stopped walking and turned to face him. Mark had fallen back like I requested. Marshon was so handsome, and he was a cool guy. In another life, maybe we could have fucked with each other, but for as cute as he was, he wasn't Fahan. Nobody was. I looked at him with tears glistening in my eyes. "I fucked up. I took that pill, I did some dumb shit, we did some dumb shit, and I'm pregnant." Marshon's eyes widened in surprise. "Kylie was there when I took the test. I know she's going to hound me to talk about it on the show, so here's the deal. I'm getting an abortion, and I'm going to tell my man once the shit airs that it was all fake."

Marshon stared at me. Stunned. Speechless. Finally, he spoke. "Um okay, I mean, I get why you feel how you feel, but we can't even have a conversation about it? You just decided on your own that's what you were gonna do and then you *tell* me. We don't discuss it?"

I narrowed my eyes at him and jerked my head back. "Discussion for what? Your rap career is taking off. You don't want a baby with me. One night of being fucked up led to a mistake, but this shit is getting fixed. ASAP."

"So what happens if you and this nigga ever break up? You might regret murdering your own seed just so he won't leave you. I'm about to be rich, and you won't be broke either. We don't have to be together to co-parent, but you won't even consider it because of a nigga."

"I'm not doing this with you. I swear to God, I'm not. When we film tomorrow, I tell you about the baby. A few weeks later, we film and say I had a miscarriage. If we can't do it like that, then fuck this show. My nigga isn't broke." I turned and walked away before Marshon could even respond. Fuck my life.

# 10

## AZAAN

"Don't fuckin' walk away from me," Vickie screamed like a lunatic and pulled on my shirt in an effort to keep me from walking out of the door.

I whirled around to face her and the only thing keeping me from going off was the fact that my son was watching us. I'd spent the last four days getting Vickie and my son moved into a new house. Shit was putting me way behind with my club, and on top of that, my aunt had called me three times crying that Meer was missing. I hadn't had the time or the heart to call Jayda, so I was sure she felt like I was doing her dirty. Shit was all fucked up and now that I was trying to get back to North Carolina to the club, Vickie wanted to act an ass. My eyes darted over to my son who had stopped watching TV and was focused on me and his mother.

I spoke through clenched teeth. "I've missed two business meetings dealing with this bullshit that could have all been avoided if it wasn't for your lying, sneaky ass. My aunt is going crazy because she thinks her son is missing. You made Meer comfortable with thinking he called the shots. You caused this shit. I had to fix it, and now I'm going to tend to my club."

"Fuck that club!" Vickie cried with tears streaming down her face. "You'd rather run back to North Carolina than to fix shit with me? You're going back to that bitch," she screeched, crying all hard.

Aheem ran over to us. "You okay Mommy?"

My nostrils flared as he looked up at his mother with worry etched on his tiny face. I licked my lips and picked him up. "Mommy is good my mans. Watch TV like a big boy." I placed a kiss on his forehead and placed him on the couch. I then walked back over towards Vickie. "Follow me."

I walked to the hallway and Vickie followed. As soon as we were out of my son's sight, I wrapped my hand around her neck and pushed her back into the wall. I spoke in a hushed tone, but the venom in my voice made Vickie aware that I wasn't playing with her. "Stop causing a scene and upsetting my muhfuckin' son. From here on out, *we* aren't shit but his parents. We're done. You got that?" I let her neck go, and she cried hard but quietly. She was crying so hard, she had to put her hand over her mouth to muffle any sound. I stared at her wondering what life would be like without her as my woman, but she violated. Had she handled shit differently with Meer, my aunt wouldn't be losing her damn mind.

I left her crying in the hall, and I walked back into the living room. I said good-bye to my son and headed outside to my rental car. It was time to head back to North Carolina.

* * *

THE CLUB WAS A PRIORITY, but as soon as I touched down in North Carolina, I had to go by Jayda's. Me popping up on her might not be cool, but after days of not talking to her or seeing her, a text or phone call wouldn't suffice. It was almost 9 pm and both her G wagon and her Maserati were parked in the driveway. I sat in my car for a minute just staring at her vehicles. Since I had deaded my relationship with Vickie, it was my first time being single in a very long time. Despite all that bullshit Jayda hollered about not being capable of loving another man, I knew she was feeling the kid. I was feeling her too, but she didn't need to be hurt anymore. If I wasn't ready to go all in with her, there was a nagging voice telling me to leave her alone. That shit was going to be hard to do though.

I didn't know what it was about Jayda, but I was drawn to her. I was addicted to her ass.

I finally stopped sitting there like a sucka and got out of the car. Jayda was chill as hell and never really tripped about anything, so I wasn't sure if she'd be mad about my disappearing act or not. I would never know until I saw her face, so I stopped beating around the bush and rang the bell. Jayda answered the door a few seconds later with a shocked look on her face. Instinctively, my eyes roamed over her body, and my dick instantly stiffened at the sight of her in short black gym shorts and a black sports bra. She'd gotten her hair done in faux locs, and her face was free of make-up. Long lashes framed her eyes, and her freckles jumped out at me.

"Damn, I missed you," I confessed without meaning to. The shit fell off my lips with no effort. "I'm sorry about just popping up on you. Are you busy?"

"No, I'm not busy. Come in."

I entered her home and closed the door behind me. I walked over to Jayda, invaded her personal space, wrapped my arms around her waist, and buried my face in the crook of her neck. I breathed in, inhaling her scent. It had been too long since I smelled her or held her, and it had been less than a week. Yeah, a nigga had it bad. "I'm sorry I haven't called," I apologized before placing a soft kiss on the corner of her lips.

"Is everything okay back home?" She looked as if she was honestly concerned and not trying to be funny.

I exhaled. Jayda seemed solid, but no way in hell was I about to confess to her that my baby moms shot my cousin in my home, and I had the body disposed of. "It will be I guess. My baby moms got into some bullshit and called me to clean it up. We broke up." I searched her eyes for her reaction.

She played it cool. "I'm sorry to hear that."

"Don't be. I'm sorry there was no communication for days, but shit was super crazy. I had to find her and my son somewhere else to live. On top of that, my cousin just got out of prison, and my aunt's been calling me crying saying he's missing. Shit is crazy."

"Damn, you have had a lot going on. I hope your cousin is okay."

I elected not to speak on that. The dirt ball ass nigga was far from okay, but it was his own fault. "So you didn't miss me?"

A half-smile adorned Jayda's face. "I probably did. A little bit. I've been trying to focus on getting back into the swing of school, so I tried to be too busy to miss you."

I pecked her on the lips once, twice, then I snaked my tongue into her mouth and squeezed her ass as we kissed. She could try to resist me all she wanted to, but our chemistry was undeniable. I kissed from her neck to her ear. "How the fuck you only missed me a little bit when I missed the fuck out you?" I asked in a low voice.

Jayda wrapped her arms around my neck and smiled at me. "Man, chill out."

I could only chuckle at her lil' wanna be gangsta ass. Jayda turned serious, licked her lips, and took a step back. She busied herself with the task of undoing my belt, then unbuttoning my jeans. I watched as she pulled my semi-hard dick out of my boxer briefs with her soft, manicured hand, then she lowered herself so that she could take me into her mouth. I assumed she'd had something to drink before I came by because her mouth was cool. I let out a low moan from the sensation as she deep throated me slowly, then began to suck my dick at a steady pace. Not too slow, not too fast. Her mouth was wet as fuck in no time, and my dick was hitting the back of her throat. I grabbed a handful of her locs and pulled my lips into my mouth as I watched her head bob up and down.

Now that I'd had the pleasure of sampling both, I could say with certainty that her pussy and her head game was fire. Jayda licked up and down my shaft, then sucked on my balls coating them with salvia. By the time she went back to lightly humming on my dick, I was letting out low moans and hissing like a muhfucka. Jayda stood up and barely had time to wipe all the excess spit from around her mouth, before I was devouring her lips like a mad man. We kissed passionately as I walked her over to the couch, where I spun her around and started eating her out from behind. In no time at all, Jayda was the one moaning. Her legs were shaking as I alternated between sucking on her clit and sliding my tongue up and down her wet slit. She cried out in ecstasy as she came, and I moaned into her pussy as I gobbled her nectar up like it was honey. I was about to fuck her better than I ever had before. I didn't care that I'd actually only been single for less than twenty-four hours. I wanted Jayda, and I was gon' have her.

# JAYDA

"Hi," I stated, pleasantly surprised after Liah opened the door to her hotel room. It had been three weeks since she got shot. She'd been out of the hospital for two days, and my parents and I went in together and paid for a hotel room for her for three weeks. That shit cost a pretty penny, and I prayed that Liah would at least stay clean for a little while. She actually looked good as hell. In the three weeks that she'd been off drugs, she looked to have gained around five pounds, maybe a little more.

She'd washed her hair and slicked it up into a bun, and while she was in the hospital, I'd brought her some face wash, and some whitening toothpaste and whitening strips. I also bought her lotion, bodywash, etc. Liah let me into her hotel room looking better than she'd looked in years. She was dressed in black leggings and a white tank top. She smelled good, and her acne was clearing up.

"Hey."

"I brought you some stuff," I said, handing her bags filled with snacks and other personal hygiene items. Liah finally told my parents that she got shot in a robbery gone wrong. She cried talking about the death of her friends, and she acted as if she really wanted to clean up her act. Hopefully this time, she was for real.

"Thank you." She took the bags and placed them on the table in her room. My dad had gotten her a cell phone. I was trying not to get my hopes up, but I knew if Liah went back to the streets it would devastate my parents. She'd never been clean for this long, even if two of those weeks she was in a coma.

"What you been up to?" I asked, sitting down. There was a slight awkwardness in the air, but I wasn't mad at Liah. Even though the shit she said pertaining to me and Biggs was mad disrespectful, I didn't hold it against her. Everything she'd done while high, I was trying to erase. If she was truly trying to change then her slate had been wiped clean with me.

"Just trying to see who's hiring. I've been googling how to do resumes and stuff, but what's the point? I don't have work experience. I don't know what I'm going to do really."

I was hesitant to let her come work at the rental place with me. You had to be very well off to rent an exotic car from Bigg Boys. I dealt with people's social security numbers, their credit card information as well as their bank information. No way was I going to give Liah access to that stuff. Not until she'd proven herself. "I'll see what I can find you. I know it's going to get boring being in this hotel room all the time." I left out the fact that boredom could lead to her linking up with old friends and associates and doing drugs.

"Tell me about it. I've rested all I could rest. I have more energy than I know what to do with." Liah looked kind of down, and that wasn't a good sign.

"Come go with me. We can hit the mall and grab some food. If you're going to be looking for a job you need some clothes, right? You'll especially need interview clothes."

Liah's eyes lit up. "You'd do that for me?"

I shrugged. "Why not? I want to see you winning. There are plenty of people that have your back. You just have to meet them halfway."

"I know. Thank you."

Liah and I left the hotel and headed to the mall. I got her a pair of slacks, a pencil skirt, three pairs of shoes, five shirts, and three pairs of jeans. She must have told me thank you five times. As we were heading for the food court, I got a text message. When I looked at my phone and saw that it was Azaan, I smiled and Liah peeped it.

"You back dating?" she inquired. "By the way, I didn't mean any of that stuff I said. I was—"

I cut her off. "It's fine Liah. You don't have to apologize, and we don't have to talk about it. I am kind of seeing someone. I don't know where it's going to go. I tried to fight it, but I like him," I admitted.

Liah gave a brief head nod. "Is it Azaan? I saw how he looked that day when I said something about you getting robbed, and he was like you're good wherever he was. He was ready to bite my head off behind you."

I tried not to smile, but I failed. "It is. Did you cop from his people often? What do you know about him?"

Liah looked away. "I don't know much. He just seems like a cool guy, and I can tell he has money. He's also handsome."

"Handsome, fine as fuck, all that," I gushed.

After what happened with Biggs, I was almost afraid to get too happy. The euphoria of everything going right will have you soaring on the highest cloud, and then one day it can all be snatched away, leaving your spirit crushed. Having Azaan in my life though and Liah being clean, it was all a dope feeling. I just had to wonder how long any of it would last.

* * *

"I HAVE A FAVOR TO ASK YOU." Later that night, Azaan and I were cuddled up in my bed watching a movie.

"What's good?" he asked in a lazy voice.

I turned around so that I was facing him. "Your club opens in a few days, right? I know the last time me, you, and my sister were around each other shit went left, but she's doing better. I told her to go to your club and apply for a job. It doesn't have to be anything that would require her to handle money. Maybe she can work in the kitchen or something. If she doesn't get a job and stay busy, I'm worried that she'll go back to drugs," I damn near pleaded with Azaan. I couldn't quite read the look on her face.

"I mean, I know she's clean, but it hasn't even been that long. You don't think she'll relapse?"

I could understand him being hesitant to give her a job. Shit, I had my own business and I wouldn't even give her a job, but as I told him, he didn't have to hire her to do anything that would require her to handle cash or people's cards. She could wash dishes or some shit. With her background, she would have to be happy with whatever she could get.

"It's always a possibility, but she's doing so good now Azaan. She's gaining weight. She actually looks healthy. My mom took her to the salon, and she got her hair cut, her skin is clearing up, I got her some new clothes. I think she really wants to do better." I told myself that if he refused to give her a job, I wouldn't be mad at him.

Azaan was a very successful businessman, and I knew he got there by making smart moves. It might not necessarily be a smart move to have an ex-junkie that hadn't even been clean for a full thirty days to work for you, but I was just trying to help her. Seeing Liah looking so good was giving me hope that she would continue to do good.

"What's in it for me?" he asked with a flirtatious smirk.

I smiled at him. "What exactly do you want?"

His gaze turned serious. "I want to be with you. I don't want the next man to ask you if you're single and you be able to tell him yes."

My heart slammed into my chest. That wasn't what I was prepared to hear. Yes, I'd let my guard down and stopped fighting my feelings for Azaan, but being his girl was something totally different. I sat up and looked down at him. I was scared to take it there with him, and there was no use in fronting about that fact. Even still, I was known in the streets as Biggs' girl. It had been four years but still, that's the title I held, and I was cool with that.

"You just got out of a relationship though," I replied lamely. That's the only thing that I could come up with that I hoped wouldn't require a lot of explanation. It was true and he knew it.

"So what? I'm not talking about that. I'm talking about us. We fuck with each other hard anyway. I been nutting all up in that pussy. We talk every day. What will be so different about us being in a relationship?"

My skin felt flushed. "Azaan, I just don't know if I'm ready for all that."

He sat up, and I hoped that our chill night wouldn't turn into an argument. "Why can't we just keep chilling like this?" I asked meekly.

Azaan stood up and reached for his jeans. "You're right. Whatever you want to do ma, that's what we'll do."

Sadness filled my eyes, but he wouldn't know that because he wouldn't even look at me as he got dressed. I didn't want him to go. Why the fuck did we have to put a title on what we were doing? Why couldn't we just chill and let the other stuff come later? "Azaan, why are you leaving?"

"I'm just gon' fall back and let you continue to do what it is that you're doing. I'll let you grieve and handle things your way without infiltrating your personal space and doing too much. I'll holla at you later." He leaned down and pecked me on the lips before grabbing his keys off my dresser and leaving.

I was pissed. I didn't even get in my feelings and make a whole scene when I found out he had a girlfriend and a kid. I had taken a huge step by even dealing with him and all of a sudden just like that, he wanted to put a title on it or he was leaving me alone? I didn't think that was fair at all, but he had a right to his feelings, I guess.

After he left, I lay back on the bed and stared up at the ceiling. I just wasn't ready to be known as anyone's girl other than Biggs.

# 12

# DIOR

"Dior you awake? You have company?" Nico peeked his head in my bedroom door. I had just woken up a few seconds before he came in. Cramps had jarred me from my sleep. I looked at my phone and saw that it was 4 pm. Five hours had passed since my abortion.

I frowned my face up from the pain in my belly and sat up. "Who is it?" I looked over at the nightstand for my pain pills.

"Marshon."

"Ugggg." My scowl deepened. I wasn't in the mood to deal with his ass. Two days prior, we'd done all the dramatic ass filming where he found out I was pregnant, and we were both supposed to be happy. In a few days, I had to go back to work and film a scene at home in bed. On camera, I would act as if the miscarriage occurred in the middle of the night while the camera crew wasn't around. I was so happy that we only had a little over a month of filming left. It was exciting at first, and I was looking forward to the checks, but lately it had become very draining. Some days I wondered if I really even wanted to be asked back for season two.

"So is that a yes or a no, bitch?" Nico asked impatiently.

"Let him in." I reached over and grabbed a bottle of water and my pain medication. I hated room temperature water, but I didn't feel like getting up.

As I was unscrewing the top on the bottle of water, Marshon eased in my room looking like a whole meal, fuck the snack. He was dressed in all white, and if this entire situation didn't have me so damn stressed, my mouth might have started to water. "So I see you went through with it huh?"

"Yeah, I did." There was a hint of attitude in my voice, and I was tired of talking about the shit. His ass couldn't want a kid that bad. He just wanted to make my life difficult. If he really wanted a child, then he could get any of the females I'm sure he was fucking pregnant. I knew they'd be more than willing.

"Well I just came to check on you. I don't know where shit went wrong with us, like there seems to be some tension. I'm not a bad guy. I presented you with an opportunity to put some money in your pocket. One night we went out, we turned up, and we had fun. We're both grown. I know you're in a relationship. Shit didn't have to get awkward after that. I feel like you're a cool female, but if you're holding your nigga down then that's what it is."

I suddenly felt bad for how I'd been treating Marshon since I got pregnant. He was right. We went out, we turned up, and we had fun. It wasn't his fault that I took the pill he gave me or even that I let him fuck me. It wasn't his fault that I didn't think about getting a plan B pill after having unprotected sex with him. It took both of us to make the child. It wasn't all his fault at all. I should have been more responsible. It was over now. I'd gotten the abortion and we could get back to the fake storylines and worry about getting to the money.

"You're right. My attitude was on the bad side, but I guess it was fear and hormones. It's over now, and we can get back to other things. So after the miscarriage, where do you think we can take our storyline?"

Marshon leaned up against my dresser, and he appeared to be in deep thought for a few minutes. "How about I plan you this big surprise party for your birthday and shit and then after that, I go out of town. You pop up on me and I have a girl in the room."

"That sounds like a plan. You remembered my birthday?" I asked him, surprised.

"Yeah, I did."

"We'll have to shoot the party the day before or the day after. I have to visit Fahan on my birthday. We're actually getting married."

Marshon raised his eyebrows. "You can't do that right now shorty."

I frowned up my face. "Why not?"

"Because once the show starts to air, people will dig into your background. They will want to know everything about you. If it comes out that you married this man *after* we started taping the show, it's gonna blow our whole shit. I'm even cool with it looking like you can't stay away from this nigga and it makes us beef. Whatever causes the drama, but you can't marry him right now. At least wait until the season has already aired."

I leaned my head back against the headboard. Even while he was in prison, technically, Fahan wasn't no broke nigga. If I told him I couldn't marry him for the show, he would demand that I quit. I couldn't do that though because I signed a contract. Shit was just all messed up. The relationship with Marshon was supposed to be fake. I never fathomed that I wouldn't be able to marry Fahan because of it. I already agreed to marry him, we set a date, he even got me a ring. How was I supposed to look him in the face and tell him we couldn't get married? It seemed as if my luck was going from bad to worse.

* * *

"WHY YOU LOOKING like that ma? What's good?" Fahan asked as he peered into my eyes. He knew me well, and he could tell that something was wrong. He'd been holding my hands in his from across the table and talking to me for the past ten minutes. I knew I appeared uncomfortable because I was, and I was doing a bad job of hiding it.

I wanted to wait until the end of our visit before I dropped the bomb on him, but there was no way I could sit in front of Fahan and try to pretend like everything was okay for two hours. I was too nervous about how he was going to take what I said. I took a deep breath and put on my big girl panties. "Fahan, baby, we can't get married on my birthday." My heart dropped at the way his face crumpled with confusion. My heart rate increased, and my hands grew clammy. "I still want to marry you, of course, but we may have to wait until the first season is done airing."

"Care to explain why?" Fahan's tone of voice was low, and he appeared calm, but the storm brewing in his eyes told me how he really felt.

I shifted in my seat. "Marshon just feels like after the show starts to air, gossip blogs and other people will be digging into my life. He feels like it won't be a good look for the show if someone finds a marriage license with a date on it for after the show began taping. Even though our story-line is fake, we signed a contract to make it appear real. I'm obligated." My eyes fell on the table in front of me once Fahan started clenching his jaw muscles together.

"Yooo, I've tried really hard to be patient with this reality show bullshit. I took into consideration that you'd be able to put some money in your pocket without having to slave at that fuck ass job. I would never try to keep you dependent on me even when I'm back out on the streets, but you're telling me that a nigga wants to marry you, and you're brushing me off for the sake of a fake relationship for TV? Where they do that at?"

Fahan had a scowl on his face that resembled one of a person sucking on a lemon. I knew he would be pissed. I guess he had a right to be. "It's just because I signed a contract. We have to at least front for the public like the relationship is real. Baby, I want to marry you more than anything." I begged with my words, my tone of voice, and my eyes for Fahan to cut me some slack. "Once you come home, I'll pay for our wedding out of my own pocket. You know I want to marry you."

Fahan slid his hands out of mine and sat back in his chair. The scowl was gone, and he looked bored. "It's all good ma. Take all the time you need and do whatever is that you need to do. We don't have to get married next month, the month after that, or the month after that."

Tears sprang to my eyes. Him being mad was something that I expected. Him not wanting to marry me anymore period broke my heart. Despite all of the mistakes that I made with Marshon, the pregnancy and all the dumb shit, Fahan was my heart. Carrying his last name would mean the world to me, but now, I may have fucked that up.

"Fahan, please don't be like that. I didn't know what I was getting myself into. I don't even want to go back for season two. Fuck that show. Once my contract is fulfilled, I'm done with it." I used the back of my hand to wipe the tears from my face.

Fahan glared at me for a minute, and then his face softened. I really fucked up if he looked at me crying and didn't melt. Fahan was a sucker for my tears. They weren't fake though. I was scared to death of losing him. I was really on the verge of saying fuck Marshon and that reality show. After about three minutes of silence, Fahan flicked the tip of his nose and sat up. "Chill with the crying," he stated in a soft voice.

"How am I supposed to feel knowing that you don't want to marry me anymore? I didn't know that having a fake relationship would be this much trouble. That's what I get for being money hungry," I whined.

Fahan placed his hand back in mine. "Chill Dior. Any female I know would have jumped at that shit. Don't beat yourself up. You know I love you, and I fuck with you. We gon' be aight."

"Fahan, I love you so much. I swear you're the best thing that ever happened to me." Despite him no longer appearing to be angry, things unknown to him had me terrified. I wasn't sure how he'd react to seeing the show once it was on air. I was starting to doubt everything, and it felt as if the walls were closing in on me. I almost hyperventilated, that's how scared I was.

Fahan tightened his grip on my hand. "Baby, we gon' be good. I promise. Stop worrying. I love the fuck out of you and there isn't shit that can change that."

# 13

## AZAAN

**M**y nostrils flared as I looked down at my ringing phone. If Vickie called me one more got damn time, I was gon' fly to Miami and choke the shit out of her. She'd called me twice and I answered and spoke to my son. When she tried to talk about us, I politely ended the call, and she'd since called me back seventeen times. She was pissing me the fuck off. I was two days away from the opening of my club, and I didn't have time to play games with her ass. She decided the fate of our relationship when she kept entertaining Meer's fuck ass behind my back and didn't feel the need to tell me about it. My aunt had gotten the police involved in Meer's disappearance. Shit was all bad, and I wanted to ring her neck every time I thought about it. She was the cause of the way the shit went down. With her lying, sneaky ass.

I wasn't in the club alone. Since we were so close to opening, I had the bartenders there familiarizing themselves with the bar. I had kitchen staff in place so they could be trained by the head cook and set up a routine to make things go smooth in the kitchen. I even had the dancers there practicing. I wasn't playing with the opening of the club. I had hired a local promoter and was pleased that all seven of my VIP booths had been booked for $700 apiece. The booth came with a complimentary dance from the stripper of their choice, a bottle of liquor of their choice, and they, of course, wouldn't have to wait in line once they arrived at the club. Bottle girls would serve them so they never had to leave their booth. I would say that $4,900 on VIP booths the opening night was a pretty good start. For our second night, I had rapper Megan Thee Stallion coming through. Four of the booths had already sold out for that night.

I was about to round everybody up for a staff meeting when the door to the club opened. I had perfect vision, but I had to do a damn double take at who I saw walking through the door. I knew that Jayda had spoken on her behalf to try and get me to hire her, but the bitch had a lot of balls coming to my place of business after what she did. Liah looked ten times better than she did the day that I shot her, but I was still able to recognize her immediately. She had picked up a few pounds and looked healthy, dressed in a black, form-fitting dress that stopped a few inches past her knee. Her face had gotten fuller, and her acne was gone. Liah had her hair cut in a bob, and she didn't have on any make-up but her eyebrows were done up how chicks be doing them, and she appeared to have on false lashes. On her feet were simple red, strappy heels. Done up, she definitely looked related to Jayda, but Jayda was still way prettier, but I was probably just biased.

Liah looked up at me nervously, and once again my nostrils flared. "You got a lot of balls coming here. Me and your sister didn't get to finish our conversation about you, but don't get that twisted to mean that I would ever fuck with you," I stated in a low tone.

"Azaan, I swear I'm sorry. When I participated in what went down, I was out here bad. I haven't done drugs in almost a month. I haven't even had a drop of alcohol. I want to do better. I swear. Jayda came to you on my behalf because she doesn't know that you're the one that shot me. If you give me a job, we can keep it like that."

I took a step towards her, and Liah flinched. "Muhfucka you threatening me? "'Cus it's nothing for me to have your ass sleeping with the fishes. Your family knows how you used to get down, so nobody will be surprised if you come up missing. First you try to rob me and now you're threatening me? You got balls bitch."

"Azaan, I don't want to come in between you and Jayda. She's been through enough. She deserves to be happy. Even before she brought up the idea of you hiring me, that reason is alone is the reason why I hadn't told her. You make her happy."

I wasn't quite sure I believed that. I mean, Biggs had been dead for four years, and shorty was still acting scared to go on with her life. I gave her good dick, and I distracted her from missing him, but if I really made her that happy, she wouldn't have hesitated to be with me. We were already strained though, and I didn't want to risk Liah's dumb ass getting in her feelings and fucking shit up for me. Jayda was probably under the impression that I was mad at her. I did feel some type of way, but I was just giving her space. It wasn't necessarily that I didn't want to fuck with her anymore, and if I killed Liah, Jayda would once again be grieving. I didn't like for anyone to threaten me, but I thought about how strongly I felt for Jayda.

"You can work in the kitchen, preparing food and washing dishes. Under no circumstances do you touch any money, and if I ever feel like you even took a napkin that you weren't entitled to, I'll put a bullet in your head faster than you can blink, and I put that on my son. The pay is $10 an hour, and you'll work Friday through Tuesday from seven pm until 3 am."

"Thank you so much Azaan. I swear I appreciate it. I know I was wrong for what I did. I did a lot of wrong to a lot of people, and I just want to make up for it."

Liah looked sincere, but I didn't trust a muhfuckin' soul that would steal from their own mother. I didn't give a damn if they were on drugs or not. She let herself become that addicted to the shit, so in my mind, she was weak. If she was that weak once, she could for damn sure be that weak again. I didn't trust her, and I would be watching her like a hawk. If Liah fucked up, her parents would be burying her. I didn't care how much I liked Jayda.

\* \* \*

"I LOVE YOUR SHOES," the brown-skinned shorty at the bowling alley came over to me and said.

I looked down at my black Louboutin sneakers. I had just arrived with Nas, Monty, and Pookie so we hadn't changed into our bowling shoes yet. The same must have applied to her because she had on Louboutin's herself. Hers were heels and they were red. My eyes roamed over her frame, and she was dressed in tight, black, ripped jeans and a red blouse. Red lipstick coated her juicy lips and her hair was in a short cut. Shorty matched my fly for real.

I licked my lips. "Thank you. Your joints is kinda sexy too," I lowkey flirted. It had been two days since I had talked to Jayda, and I missed her, but I wasn't folding. I was giving shorty her space until she decided to fuck with me. It was a day before the opening of my club, and the fellas had talked me into coming out to have drinks and chill. All I did was work, and they felt like I needed a break, if only for a few hours, and I had agreed. Nas and Monty were from Miami like me, but they both had a few chicks they'd fucked with since arriving in North Carolina. I knew they were always down to meet more. Now that I was single and Jayda was on some iffy shit, I might as well mingle and have fun too.

"Thank you. It's just you and your friends here? I'm not stepping on anybody's toes am I?" She looked around. I assumed she was trying to see if we had any women with us.

"Nah, you good shawty. Yeah, it's just me and my patnas. Who you here with?"

"Two of my homegirls. My name is Persia."

"Azaan. Nice to meet you." I extended my hand for a shake, and she smiled.

"I really hate to be forward or come off as thirsty, but is it cool if maybe we all bowl together? Do you have a girlfriend?"

I gave her a half-smile. She saw something she liked, and she went after it. I wasn't mad at that. "I'm single, and I'm sure my homies don't mind. Let me holla at them."

One glance at Persia's friends, and my niggas were with it. We bowled together as a group, and I had to admit that I had a good time. I didn't give shorty too much information about myself. I just told her that I was from Miami and in town on business. I found out that we were the same age and that she had her own accounting firm. Shorty had been divorced for two years and had five-year-old twin boys. She was cool, and at the end of the night we exchanged numbers. I had a few more months to be in North Carolina, so why not meet people and have fun? There were women out here that knew exactly what they wanted, so why dwell on somebody that wasn't sure? Life was too short for that shit, and I'm that muhfuckin' nigga. I tried to do right, but if being a bachelor and bedding different women was the lifestyle that the Universe was leading me to, then that's just what it was.

# JAYDA

"**Y**eah, I gathered up mad clothes in my closet that still had the tags on them and gave them to my brother. It was probably about five hundred dollars' worth of clothes. He fell on hard times, so I didn't mind."

I raised one eyebrow as my date, Carl, spoke about some shit I couldn't have cared less about. I looked over at Deeanna who was sitting across the table from me, and she mouthed the words *sorry*. She knew Carl was getting on my nerves, but I was taking one for the team. She and Simon had broken up like they normally did every few months, and the guy that she was going out with, wanted to double date with his best friend. I guess because I'd entertained Azaan, Deeanna felt like I was ready to jump back out there, and she begged me to attend. I decided to do it, and I was regretting every second of it.

Carl was very handsome, he was dressed nice, and he smelled wonderful. I could tell from his manicured nails and stark white teeth that he was a man that took pride in his appearance. He also pulled up driving a 2017 Range Rover, and I wasn't mad at that. But baby was cocky as fuck and an arrogant narcissist. The entire night he talked about what he had, what he was going to buy, or what he bought for others. The man was full of himself, and I wasn't impressed. I was so ready for dinner to be over that it wasn't even funny. I wasn't even sure how we got on the subject of his brother falling on hard times. I had done a lot for my sister, but you wouldn't find me telling a stranger that over dinner. He just wasn't my type, and no one could pay me to go on a second date with him.

The entire time that he spoke, I found my mind drifting towards thoughts of Azaan. He hadn't reached out to me, and I hadn't reached out to him, but I knew it was the night that his club opened. I also knew that he'd taken a chance and given my sister a job. I wanted to text him and thank him just for that alone, but I had decided against it. Once the waiter brought the check over, I decided on a whim that I would swing by his club and support. I was dressed in a pink sleeveless dress that stopped inches above my knees. I also had on gold heels, so I could get into a club without feeling too awkward. On the way out of the restaurant, Carl asked for my number, and I made sure to give him the wrong one. Deeanna walked me to my car, and as soon as we were out of earshot, she erupted into laughter.

"Oh my god, I am so sorry. I could tell by the look on your face that he was getting on your last nerve. Thank you so much for doing this for me." She stretched her arms wide for a hug.

I rolled my eyes upwards. "No problem, and just know that I will never do it again. That nigga was the worst date in the history of dates," I stated with a frown on my face.

"Trust me, it could have been worse. He could have done some fuck boy shit like asked you to split the tab with him. Anyway, thank you for coming. What you about to get into?"

I decided to be honest. "I'm going to the club to say hello to Azaan. It opened tonight."

Deeanna's eyes opened wide. "Ohh, that sounds like fun. I'm going to see if Robert wants to go with me, but I will make it clear that Carl cannot come."

I giggled. "You do that. I don't even plan to stay long. I just want to support." I bit my bottom lip nervously. I missed Azaan terribly, but if he wasn't feeling me at the moment, there wasn't anything I could do about it.

"Okay, well I'll see what he says. I'll text you in a bit."

"Cool."

I got in my car and thought about how I woke up crying that morning. I had dreamed about Biggs and though I would always love and remember him, I just wanted the grieving to be over. How long was I going to cry? How long was I going to be afraid to give myself to another man completely? I wished I had control over it, but the fact of the matter was that I didn't. What was even worse was the fact that I had fallen for someone that I wasn't so sure it was safe to fall for. Azaan had a child with a woman. He had history with her. Break ups didn't mean shit. Some couples break up just to make-up. It's what they're good with. Handing my heart over to a man whose heart belonged to another woman seemed dumb as fuck, but I couldn't shake Azaan. If I wasn't dreaming about Biggs, then I was thinking about Azaan. The shit was crazy.

As soon as I pulled up at Azaan's club, I got a text from Deeanna saying that she and Robert were coming in about fifteen minutes. I was glad that I didn't have to be there alone. I stared at the club. I was happy for Azaan. It was only 10 pm, and the parking lot was almost packed which was a good thing. Most clubs didn't start jumping until midnight or a little later. I pulled lip gloss from my purse and freshened up my lips. I then checked my hair and made sure that I looked okay. After popping a piece of gum into my mouth, I headed for the club entrance. Thankfully, there wasn't a line, and I didn't have to wait. I saw a sign on the door that said for opening night, ladies got in free. Once I was inside, I headed for the packed bar as I observed my surroundings. The club was full of men, and as I walked to the bar, I received plenty of cat calls and men trying to stop me by gently pulling my arm as I walked by, but I kept moving. I wasn't there for any of it.

At the bar, I waited patiently for my turn. After I ordered a double shot of Patrón, I continued to watch. There was a beautiful light-skinned woman on the stage that had a humongous ass. She was at the top of the pole hanging upside down, and money littered the stage. "Here you go boo.

That'll be thirteen dollars," the bartender called out to me, snapping me from my thoughts.

I handed her the money and placed a tip in the jar. After two big swallows, my glass was empty, and a warm, fuzzy feeling was coursing through my body. A few men came up to me trying to make small talk and I politely and respectfully declined all advances. After about thirty minutes of being in the club, I spotted Azaan. My breath caught in my throat as I saw him near the stage talking to a pretty brown-skinned woman. She was touching him flirtatiously, and I cocked my head slightly to the left as I studied them. He was so damn fine, and I knew women probably tried to get at him every day. For whatever reason, he wanted me, and I was bullshitting. I watched as he flashed his winning smile. Shorty was batting her eyelashes and moving in close as she spoke. I mean, she was doing the most, but I couldn't blame her not one bit.

I turned back to the bar and ordered another shot of Patrón. As I turned back around, Azaan looked up and our eyes locked. I smiled at him. I wanted him to know that no matter what, I was proud of him. He stared at me for so long that the woman he'd been speaking to looked over at me. She was no doubt trying to see what had his attention. Just as the bartender handed me my drink, Azaan said a few words to ole girl before leaving her looking disappointed and heading in my direction.

Azaan came over just as the bartender was handing me my change. "Give her money back. Anything she orders is on me," Azaan stated to the short girl behind the bar.

"Azaan, no. Let me support your business the way you support mine," I said in a soft voice.

He turned to look at me. "Nah. I appreciate the gesture, but nah. Thank you for coming."

I stared at him. He was so handsome and so perfect. "You're welcome," I answered before throwing back my shot.

"What you drinking? I'll get you a bottle of that shit."

I smiled. "I def don't need a whole bottle of Patrón. Well maybe I do, because Deeanna and her date are coming through." As if on cue, she texted me and told me they were at the door.

Azaan told the bartender to get me a bottle of Patrón. The tequila had me feeling good as fuck. So good that it didn't bother me that old girl was glaring at us. If Azaan had left me to talk to another woman, I'd probably be glaring too. I felt good. Good enough to confess some shit to him. "Azaan, I miss you."

He looked down at me. "Word?"

"Yes. And I miss more than your dick." That got a smile out of him. "Whatever you want to do, I'm with it." The tequila had me throwing caution to the wind and saying fuck it. Azaan made me happy. Trying to fight it wouldn't do a damn thing to change that fact.

"So you ready to be mine?" he asked with hope in his eyes.

"I am," I answered as I saw Deeanna and Robert headed in my direction.

Azaan kissed me on the lips. "You better mean that shit," he spoke into my ear.

I gazed into his eyes. "I do mean it." Maybe in the middle of a packed and noisy club wasn't the best place to confess my feelings, but fuck it. It was what it was.

Azaan gripped my waist and looked at me as if I was the only other person in the room besides him. "This is quite the nice establishment you have here," Deeanna shouted over the music, interrupting the intimate moment I was having with Azaan.

He thanked her, and the next two hours I had a blast. We drank, we danced, we tipped the strippers, we took pictures, and I laughed until my stomach hurt. It was the most fun that I'd had in a very long time. At the end of the night, I stayed with Azaan while he shut everything down. I was drunk as fuck and the chicken wings, collard greens, and macaroni and cheese that I'd had from the kitchen had me full as hell and ready to sleep like a baby. I'd even peeked in the kitchen and saw Liah working hard. My heart swelled with pride as she moved around the kitchen fixing orders. She didn't even know I was watching her.

Azaan refused to let me drive so he drove my car and left his parked at the club. We pulled up at his house, and I couldn't wait to take my clothes off and get in the bed. I was drunk as a skunk. Azaan told me he was going to take a shower and no lie, before he could even turn the shower on, I was underneath his covers with my eyes closed. I dozed off in no time, but soon my eyelids were fluttering open, and I was moaning as Azaan's tongue swirled around my clit. I arched my back and slightly raised my hips to feed myself to him. His mouth felt so good on my pussy.

Every time his tongue grazed my clit, I let out a soft moan. He ate my pussy slowly and precisely. Azaan gripped my ass as he ate me out and had my legs shivering and my pussy creaming. He stopped just before I had an orgasm and before I could protest, he covered my mouth with his and stuffed his dick all in me. I screamed into his mouth as I came hard as fuck. "This my pussy?" he spoke into my mouth as we continued to kiss. My juices were coating his dick and running out of my pussy.

"Ummmhmmm," I whimpered as he began to fuck me hard and fast.

My breasts bounced up and down and Azaan's balls smacked into my ass as he pounded in and out of me savagely. I damn near bit my tongue he was fucking me so hard. Azaan pushed one of my legs all the way back and proceeded to dig my back out while my toes touched his headboard.

"Fucckkk," he moaned as he stirred my middle.

He flipped me over so that I was on top and I took the opportunity to be in control. I didn't move right away. With his dick just in me, I leaned down and kissed the corner of his lips. I then sucked on his earlobe and then his neck. Right when his breathing became labored, I moved my hips in a slow wind and began to ride him. Azaan's hands rested on my ass as I did my thing. He fucked me hard and fast, and I was riding him nice and slow. I enjoyed the sounds of his deep moans. My clit swelled, and I felt that familiar sensation brewing in my belly. I sped up the pace as I anticipated the orgasm that was to come. Azaan lifted me up and down on his dick by my ass. "Cum on that dick baby," he urged as I pinched my nipple.

I did just as he asked, and the floodgates opened leaving me breathless and spent. Azaan flipped me over once again, but that time I was flat on my stomach. He eased into me from behind and fucked the taste out of my mouth for ten more minutes before he was erupting inside of me. Between the Patrón and the way that Azaan put it on me, I was out for the count right there in the last position that we fucked in.

* * *

THAT MORNING, as soon as I opened my eyes, I groaned. I had overdone it with the Patrón. What made me feel so good and hype the night before, now had me queasy and extremely tired. I needed lots of water but not on an empty stomach. As if my senses were synchronized with my thoughts, the aroma of food immediately filled my nostrils. Looking around Azaan's room, I could only surmise that he was in the kitchen cooking. My mouth tasted horrible, and I sat up to find my purse. I was glad that I always kept an extra toothbrush on me. I had braces as a teenager and grew accustomed to brushing my teeth after every meal.

As I brushed my teeth, I thought about how I'd promised to be Azaan's girl. There was no turning back, and I just hoped that I wouldn't come to regret the decision. It was time for me to put my big girl panties on and move on. I could do it, and if it ended badly then oh well, that was life. I could bounce back from anything. Once my teeth were brushed, I hopped in the shower. After washing my body, drying off, and putting lotion on, I rummaged around in Azaan's drawer for a tee shirt and some boxer briefs to put on. I'd put my dress back on before I left but until then, I wanted to be comfortable.

I wandered into the kitchen and found him piling food onto plates. It looked and smelled delicious, and my stomach growled loud as hell. Azaan looked over at me and smiled. "You hungry?" He chuckled.

"And hungover." I stood beside him with a pout on my face. "I am never drinking Patrón again."

Azaan handed me my plate and kissed me on the lips. "You'll be aight. I got some Gatorade in the fridge. You want blue or red?"

"Red." I shoveled a forkful of eggs into my mouth, closed my eyes and moaned. "Oh my god, these are good." I bit into a piece of turkey bacon and moaned, causing Azaan to laugh.

"Am I really nice like that or are you just that hungry?"

I smiled. "You're really nice like that." I stared at him as he opened the Gatorade for me and placed it down beside my plate. He really was a good ass catch. He was so damn fine that I could stare at him all day. He was super sweet and that made me want to kiss on him, love on him, and just be mad affectionate all day. I wondered if it would stay that way. Once the honeymoon phase was over in a lot of relationships, you really got to see a person's true colors. I hoped the Azaan that I had fallen for would be the same Azaan in two or three years. Would he and his baby mama get back together?

I shook off my doubts and worries and went back to eating my food.

"What you got planned for the day?" he asked.

"Nothing much. I think this is the first Saturday that I took off in a long time. I guess I'll go home and clean and find something to do."

"Or you can chill with me. I gotta go pick up some money and after that, I'm chilling until I have to be at the club tonight. We can do something."

"That sounds good. So ummm," my voice trailed off, and I sipped from my drink. "Now that we're official, what about the fact that you're going back to Miami?"

Azaan shrugged one shoulder. "What about it? I'm my own boss, so traveling is nothing for me. I can do a week there and then a week here. I mean, North Carolina is cool, but my son is in Miami. The time that I'm in Miami, you can come with me whenever you want. Even though when you're a big time lawyer, you might not be able to travel back and forth like that. We'll work it out though."

He said it as if it was no big deal, but I wasn't sure. When he was in Miami for a week and if I did have work or school, I'd be worried that he was with his ex or another woman. Azaan sensed my doubt. "Chill, we have a few more months before we have to worry about that."

I decided that he was right. There was no use in worrying today about something that was months away. Plus, he was right. Even after school started, I'd be free on Friday, Saturday, and Sunday. Miami was an hour away by plane. I could fly out Thursday night and stay until Sunday night. I didn't have to be up under Azaan every second of every day. It would be okay if we didn't see each other for two or three days. I could live with that. As far as being able to trust him, I refused to be one of those nagging ass, insecure girlfriends. Until he gave me a reason not to trust him, then I was just going to chill. Only time would tell if he would remain true.

# 15

## FAHAN

"Here," Simone said, discreetly pulling a piece of folded up paper from her pocket.

I looked up curiously from the magazine that I was reading. "What's this?"

"It's a contract that I printed up for you to sign. So far, I've typed up ten chapters of your book, and I have thirteen more to go. I went ahead and sent the first three chapters into a publishing company, and they loved it Fahan." Simone's eyes were lit up like a Christmas tree. I looked over the paper not even really processing what she was saying. "They want to sign you. I spoke to them and let them know your situation and the publisher is even willing to give you a $1,000 up front signing bonus."

My eyes scanned over the paper, and I saw that the publisher wanted me to sign with him for six books. Writing was just something that I did in prison because I was bored. I never thought it would lead to legit income, but even with Azaan getting the club for us, this might be a way to ensure that I never had to step back into the drug game. I never wanted to come back to prison, and I for sure wanted more money than I'd be able to spend. Maybe this was a stepping stone. I had two more books done, so that would just mean I'd have to write three more to give the publisher. I looked up at Simone, and she was smiling.

"Damn, that's what's up. What I owe you for doing this for me?" She took the time to type the book, and she reached out on my behalf, so surely she'd want a cut of the thousand dollars. I didn't mind though.

"I don't want anything except for you to be successful. Hurry up and sign the paper, so I can get out of here. You know niggas are nosey."

I was shocked to say the least. These days everybody had a motive. If Simone truly didn't want anything from me, that made her even more dope in my eyes. I read through the paper as fast as I could. I knew she needed me to hurry, but I wasn't signing shit without knowing all of the details. Fuck that shit. Even if I didn't make a lot of money, at least I could put forth the effort. If I saw a check for $200 that would be the first legit money that I made on my own, and I'd be proud of myself. Shit, maybe once the reality show aired and Dior got her followers up, some of them would fuck with my book. I never needed to ride anyone's coattails, but if we did this the right way, it could make us rich. I wanted to give her the world anyway for holding a nigga down. Just the thought of being able to buy her a new car and put her in a big ass crib excited me.

Once I made sure that everything looked good, I signed my name and handed the paper back to Simone. "Thank you for doing this for me."

"You don't have to thank me. You're very talented, and once they let you out of here, I never want to see you in here again."

Simone walked out of my cell, and I sat there smiling like a goofy. In the entire time that I'd been in prison, I had only smiled maybe once or twice, if you didn't include visits with Dior. There wasn't a damn thing to smile about in prison. Not even funny shit on TV made me laugh. I hated my living conditions, and I just kept my head down and minded my business. Thank God I had a little hustle and I had a brother that kept my books straight. If I had to survive solely on food from the kitchen, I'd be a skeleton. I ate straight from the commissary, and with the money that Azaan sent me, I ate damn good.

I hadn't written anything in almost a week but after signing that contract, I grabbed my notebook and began to write. I was motivated. I could for sure have three books done by the time I got out of prison and that way once I was out, I could just concentrate on the club. I was determined to make Azaan proud. I knew I fucked up big time when I dropped out of college and then got a charge. I needed to make it up to him and prove to him and myself that I was more than just a screw up.

I was young so I still had some traveling and living to do but after another year or two, my plans were to pump Dior full of babies. I wanted three kids, two boys and a girl. I wrote my ass off for about an hour then I had to stop and take a break because my hands were starting to cramp up. I looked up at the clock and saw that it was almost 5 pm. I decided to wait until around seven to call Dior, since she might still be filming. Just as I was about to look through my food stash and decide what to cook in the microwave, another CO by the name of Watts appeared at my cell door.

"Cezar, Ms. Johnson wants to see you."

I didn't ask any questions, but my face held a curious expression. Ms. Johnson was my counselor. We rarely talked because we didn't really have a reason to. I wondered if I was in some kind of trouble but then again if I was, I'd be getting called into the Sargent's office. I followed him down the long corridor to the office of the young, blonde haired counselor. The man in me could tell you that shorty was bad, but I didn't like white girls, so I never looked too hard. But I hadn't had pussy in so long that if she offered it to me, I'd take the shit. It's all the same color when the lights go out. I looked at her big, perky breasts and licked my lips. I bet she was a freak too.

"Hi Mr. Cezar. Have a seat. This won't take long because it's actually time for me to get off, but I didn't want to wait until tomorrow to tell you."

Okay, now I was really interested. Shorty clasped her hands together and gave me a big smile. "I got a call from a higher up today, and it seems that you are being released in fourteen days."

I raised one eyebrow. As far as I knew, I was the only Cezar at the prison, but maybe she had me fucked up with somebody else. I had a little less than four months left on my sentence. I didn't have a lawyer working on my behalf, so I was very confused. "Why am I getting out in fourteen days?"

She opened the folder on her desk and looked down at the documents inside. "It seems that they miscalculated your time served in the county jail. Add in the fact that you're a non-violent offender and you haven't had any infractions since you got here, and ta da. Someone favors you."

I didn't know what in the hell to say. I was scared that if I got too excited that she'd come back within the next few days and tell me that there had been some sort of mistake. I didn't even want to call Dior and give her the good news then have to call her back and tell her it was a mistake. A nigga would love nothing more than to go home in the next fourteen days, but it was too soon to be getting my hopes up.

"I guess so," I replied in a voice laced with skepticism.

As much as I wanted to keep the news to myself, I had to call Azaan. I knew that if anyone had moved on my behalf it would have to have been him. Once he answered and accepted the call, he spoke into the phone. "What up lil' bruh?"

"Aye, have you spoken to anyone about me? Like a lawyer or anything?" I fished for information.

"I spoke to quite a few people. Why, what's good?"

I almost got excited. "Why didn't you tell me? Who did you speak to?"

Azaan chuckled. "Like I said, I spoke to quite a few people. Money talks and bullshit walks. So what's good? You got a nigga in suspense and shit."

I smiled wide as fuck. Wider than I had smiled in a very long time. Once again my big brother came through. I owed him so much. "They told me I'm coming home in fourteen days." I grinned into the phone. Whatever he had done, I was grateful as shit.

"That's what the fuck I'm talking about," Azaan roared. "I'm 'bout to go shopping for you right now. You gon' come home to a gang of shit. What sizes you wear?"

All I could do was shake my head. Being that they were in another country, I could only talk to my dad, grandma, and other siblings through letters. I missed my mom every day, but a nigga was far from alone. Azaan and Dior made sure of that. He was the best brother that a nigga could ask for and I was even more determined to come home and make him proud. As much as I wanted to shout the good news from the roof tops, I decided that no one else would know of my release. I was going to surprise the shit out of Dior.

# 16

## AZAAN

I headed towards my home in Miami with a smile on my face. I was about to spend some time with my son. The night before had been my club's fifth night in business and shit was lovely. At the rate that it was going, I'd be seeing a profit in about four months. Much sooner than I had expected with all the money that I put in it and paying a few celebrities to come do shows and host parties and shit. In exactly eight days, my brother would be a free man. I had already hit the mall and copped him ten outfits, socks, drawers, and shoes. I spent a little over $7,000 in the mall, and I didn't have to think twice about it. Lil' bruh was gon' walk up out them gates and come home knowing that I was gon' ride for him until the wheels fell off. Nas was home visiting too, so I was going to get him to drive one of my whips back so that Fahan could use it until he got his own car.

Being that the club was new, I was hesitant to leave, but I was missing the fuck out of my son. I was spending three days in Miami, so Jayda had agreed to hold the club down for me. Everything about shorty was so perfect. Even with her flaws, I was really glad that I met her. She made a nigga happy. She was part of the reason I hadn't come back to Miami and put my foot in Vickie's ass. Her and my son. They were keeping me sane because Vickie was testing my gangsta. She was texting me all kinds of dumb shit once she saw that I was really done with her. Bitch even said she was going to sell my club, since it was in her name. I knew she was trying to get my attention, but Vickie had to know that her committing suicide would be safer than playing with me.

I was tired as hell. I'd spent a grip on a house that I'd never even slept in. As I pulled up in the driveway, I glanced at the clock on my dashboard and saw that it was damn near 10 pm. More than likely, my son was sleep, but he was going to be happy as hell waking up to my face. I was spending three whole days with him before heading back to North Carolina. Even though Vickie and I weren't on good terms, I was considering asking her to bring him to Charlotte once Fahan was released. He wouldn't be able to leave the city, and I wanted him to get to know his only nephew. Just like I wanted my son to know his uncle. I just didn't want Vickie in North Carolina on no dumb shit. I didn't want her and Jayda beefing. She fucked up, and the next female took her nigga. No need for her to be salty about it.

I was so tired that I decided to leave my bag in the car and get it in the morning. As I walked up in the driveway, my eyebrows crumpled in confusion at the red Benz that was parked in front of one of Vickie's cars. Her sister didn't have a Benz, and Vickie knew how I felt about random muhfuckas being in my crib. I peeped the New York tags on the car and the dark tints, and I went right back to my car and pulled my gun from underneath the seat. Whoever was in my crib was getting the fuck out if I had never met them personally. I didn't want to hear no sob stories about no homegirls, gym partners, none of that shit. Vickie was already skating on thin ice. Just because I was out of town didn't mean she could lose her mind and start disobeying the rules that I had for my crib. I stuck my key in the door and pushed it open. There were no lights on in the living room, and it was quiet as hell in the front of the house. That really piqued my interest, but I still gave Vickie the benefit of the doubt and decided she must be in the movie room. The potent smell of marijuana invaded my nostrils as I headed down the hallway towards the movie room, only to find the shit was empty.

My nostrils flared, and I gripped the gun that was in my hand as I headed for my bedroom. I didn't want to catch another body. I swear I didn't, but I would. When I reached my bedroom, the door was closed, and I took a deep breath to brace myself for what was to come. Vickie had better be in there with another woman getting her pussy sucked or some shit. I heard a moan, and my blood began to boil with rage. I pushed the bedroom door open, and damn near lost my mind as I saw a nigga in the bed that I bought, with Vickie's legs on his shoulders. He was fucking her so hard that the headboard was slamming into the wall and they hadn't even heard me come in the room.

I approached the bed and hit that nigga in the back of the head with my gun so hard that he fell forward and his face hit the headboard. Vickie screamed and when she saw me standing there, she looked as if she'd seen the devil himself. I'd deal with her later. Before ole boy could get himself together, I put one knee on the bed so I could get to him, and I hit him in the head and the face with my gun over and over and over again. I damn near blacked out. I faintly heard Vickie crying, but she did the shit. When she decided to be bold enough to fuck a nigga in my bed, she unknowingly agreed to be responsible for the consequences. This lame ass nigga had to know she had a dude. I know he didn't think she copped the crib and all those whips her damn self.

When I finally stopped beating ole dude, his face was a bloody mess, and he was barely breathing. I wasn't trying to kill him. I didn't need to have to dispose of another body. "Where the fuck is my son?" I asked, out of breath.

"In-in his r-room. He's asleep."

I glared at her. "You freak ass bitch. You fucking another nigga in my crib, in my bed, while my son is here? You done violated so many times that right now, it's nothing but God keeping you breathing. But grab ya nigga and get the fuck out my crib. Leave the car keys and anything else you own."

Vickie's eyes widened. "Azaan, please don't do that. You broke up with me, and I'm sad and lonely. It was stupid to bring him here, but baby, I'm sorry. I don't want to take Aheem out and—"

"Oh nah, my son not going nowhere. I got him. You go with this nigga."

The dude in my bed was struggling to get up. The sheets were ruined, but I didn't want them anymore anyway. When I did move back to Miami, I was going to get a whole new bed. No telling how many times her bird ass had fucked in it while I was away. Vickie had really tried her best to treat me like a simp ass nigga.

"Don't make me leave my baby. Please Azaan. I'm begging you," Vickie cried with snot pouring from her nose.

I cocked my gun and put it to her head. "When he gets older, you want me to have to tell him how I walked in and found you dead after this nigga murked you?"

Vickie knew I was capable of doing just that. She was already dead to me, so why not make it official? She jumped up out of the bed and looked around on the floor for her clothes.

"Nah shorty. Leave naked," I stated in a menacing tone.

Vickie parted her lips, but no words came out. She knew my patience was wearing very thin with her. I never in my life thought that Vickie and I would be reduced to this. I was so mad that I could have spit nails, but my son was in the house. Even if he was asleep, I had to be smart about how I moved. I didn't need him waking up to police crawling everywhere. I didn't want this place to be a crime scene. It had to be Vickie's lucky day. Still crying, she got the nigga up out of the bed and helped him out of the bedroom. He was disoriented and leaking blood. So now my tired ass had to at least get the blood up off the floor and take the sheets off the bed. I was going to sleep on the couch. As mad as I was, I probably wouldn't get any sleep. Vickie had really tried my ass. I was even surprised that I let her get away with her life.

* * *

I FINALLY DOZED off around two in the morning after several shots of vodka and a blunt. I woke up at 6 in the morning to the sun peeking through the windows and my phone ringing. I let out a tired breath and squinted my eyes at my bright ass phone screen. I wasn't sure why Vickie's mom was calling me because there wasn't shit she could tell me about her disrespectful, cum guzzling freak of a daughter.

"Hello?" I sat up and wiped sleep from my eyes.

"Azaan, you know for the most part, I try to stay out of anything pertaining to you and Vickie, but the fact that she showed up here in the middle of the night with no clothes on is disturbing to me. And you wouldn't let her get her son?"

"It was disturbing to me to walk up in the house that I paid a grip for and finding your slut of a daughter fucking another nigga in the custom made bed that my money paid for. The disrespect was too real, and you should be happy that I didn't kill her ass."

Vickie's mother gasped at my words, but I didn't care. Her daughter had tried it. I'm a respectful person until I'm disrespected. She messed up by calling me trying to advocate for her daughter. There was nothing she could ever tell me to make me sorry for what I'd done.

"I get that you are upset, and you have every right to be. I love my daughter Azaan, and I will tell her to stay away from you because what you just said was real wrong." Her voice cracked and she began to cry. "You're not perfect. We've all made mistakes, and no matter what Vickie has done, she loves her son. Don't take him from her."

"Well Vickie is homeless, so if she can have proper living arrangements before I go back to North Carolina, then I'll consider it. Staying with you won't really be an option. Why should my son have to go from having his own room to sharing a room with his mother? You only have a two bedroom right?"

Vickie's mother sighed. "She can have a place in three days. Just please give her time."

"Cool. Until then, I'll be spending time with my son." I ended the call and got up to take a shower and cook my lil' man breakfast. Any love that I had for Vickie was gone. I wasn't playing when I said she was dead to me, and if she thought she could play with my son, she was gon' end up dead for real.

# 17

# LIAH

"**T**his is nice," I stated, looking around the dimly lit restaurant. Being sober was like being in a whole 'nother world.

"Yeah, I heard the food here is really good," my date replied.

I hadn't been sober in my adult years so going out on dates and shit was foreign to me. The only thing I ever did with guys was get high and fuck. I wasn't on social media or anything. It's like once I started doing drugs, I started living my life in a bubble. Of course, people that had seen me over the years knew that I was out there bad, but not everyone knew. When I got back on social media and posted a few pictures, my DMs started going crazy. One of my classmates, a guy named Derrin, was back from living in New Jersey for a while, and we started chatting through messenger. After a few days of that, he asked for my number and then he asked me out.

Before Azaan shot me, I was one hundred and five pounds. I was currently at one hundred thirty-five pounds. I had filled out very nicely. I went to the dentist and got my teeth cleaned, I deep conditioned my hair once a week and was putting vitamin E oil in it, so it was getting thick and healthy. I was dressed in a peach-colored romper, and I felt really good about myself. I had a job, and even though Azaan often looked at me like he hated me, I thanked God for it. My job kept me busy. When I wasn't working, I was asleep, on social media, browsing the internet, or talking to my parents or Jayda. I had been clean for more than a month and as a present, my dad paid the security deposit on an apartment for me. I told him that I wanted to pay the first month's rent myself, and he told me if I did that, he'd buy me a bedroom set. I hadn't even had the desire to do any drugs, but I knew it was because I had a good support system. I knew the day would come when something would piss me off or make me sad or frustrated, and it would be in those moments that I'd be the most tempted to use again.

In an effort to keep myself on the right track, I'd just think about sleeping in a car in the dead of winter and freezing my ass off. I'd think about the way I smelled after not bathing for four or five days because I had nowhere to go. I'd think about both my friends being dead. Making my own money and getting myself together was a better high than being a lowlife fiend. I refused to ever go back to that way of living. I liked working at the club but if I wanted to be able to pay rent, get a car, etc., I'd need more than ten dollars an hour. Once I'd been working there for a while, I planned to apply for some other places. I heard of a few warehouses and call centers that started people out at around $15 an hour with the ability to do overtime.

The hostess seated me and Derrin, and I thought back to high school. He was a popular ass jock that looked down on girls like me because of the people that I hung around. I often had to remind myself that we were grown now, and he definitely seemed to have matured. He worked at a car lot, and he seemed like a very humble guy. The opposite of what he'd been in high school. He didn't have kids and was divorced. He told me that after only being married for a year, his wife cheated on him and left him for the guy that she cheated with.

"So you said on the phone your last relationship was high school?" he asked, making conversation.

I picked up my glass of water and took a sip. Over the years, I couldn't be sure who had seen me out high and looking a hot mess. I wasn't sure how far Derrin and I would get or if he would ever run into anyone that would tell him about my past, but I just didn't want to tell him that at one point,

I'd been strung out on coke, ecstasy, and sometimes molly. My main thing was coke. I snorted coke two to three times a day and smoked it in weed at least once a day to give my nose a break from the constant sniffing. A few times I tried coke in hard form (crack) but that shit had me geeked out of my mind. I didn't really like smoking crack but if I couldn't get my hands on any soft, then I'd smoke it hard.

Some days I gave coke a break, but I would take ecstasy or molly to try and keep the withdrawal symptoms at bay. Long story short, not a day went by for years that I wasn't high off something. I decided to downplay the situation. "I spent my years after high school rebelling and being a wild child. My parents were constantly kicking me out, I was staying with different friends, shit was a mess. I didn't have the maturity or the mindset to be in a relationship. All the crowd that I ran with wanted to do was smoke weed and do dumb shit."

Derrin nodded. "I can get that. I'm glad you got it together. Life is about learning from our experiences. You're just working at the club now?"

"Yeah. I thought long and hard about it, and I want to enroll in school to be a dental hygienist assistant."

Derrin nodded in approval. "I think that's dope. You should go for it."

"I think I am."

"You working tonight?"

"Yeah, I am. The club is cool. It keeps me busy."

Dinner was cool and conversation with him flowed very easily. I did have to go to work, so we cut the date short and he dropped me off at the hotel so I could get changed and take an Uber to work. I really hated starting off whatever we were doing with a lie, but I didn't tell him the real reason that I was staying at a hotel. I told Derrin that when my lease was up, I was in between jobs so my parents got me a hotel room. I talked more than once to him about the fact that our relationship used to be strained and that I just didn't want to live in the same house with them. I hoped that he bought it. Nothing would run a man away faster than telling him that you used to be an addict that stole from your parents and tried to rob your sister's boyfriend's trap house and then he shot you. I just wanted to keep all of that to myself. Maybe if we continued to talk to one another I could one day tell him the truth and he wouldn't judge me for it.

I headed for work in the Uber thinking about how much my life had changed in the past month. I was clean, and I had a job. I'd never worked before in my life. I moved non-stop from the time I clocked in until the time that I clocked out. Azaan's club was packed almost every night, and orders came to the kitchen back to back. I always got off work exhausted, and that's what I needed. I would get back to the hotel, shower, and be out like a light. The head cook for the club was a woman in her early fifties, and she could cook her ass off. I ate from the club at least three nights a week, and I made sure to always let the bartender ring me up, and I kept my receipt. The last thing I wanted was for Azaan to think I was stealing. I couldn't even be mad at the fact that he didn't like me. I had violated in a major way, and I knew I had to pay for what I'd done. I was just glad that I didn't pay for it with my life.

When I arrived at the club, there were only a few cars sprinkled in the parking lot, and they all belonged to staff. The kitchen crew came in at seven to start prepping the food and getting ready for the night. The club opened at nine, and as soon as people started piling in, the orders started coming. Most people didn't order food until they were about to leave the club. Some people actually paid the cover charge just to come in and order some food. It was just that good. I stayed in the kitchen my entire shift, even during my break. I only left if I had to use the bathroom. It didn't bother me that people were in the same building as me getting drunk and high. Sometimes I got tempted to drink some wine, and maybe one day I would. For the moment, I was content with being sober though.

I thanked the Uber driver and got out of the car. As I headed up to the entrance of the club, I noticed a guy standing outside smoking a cigarette, but I didn't recognize him as staff. He looked up at me, and I remembered who he was instantly. He smiled at me, but I knew we were far from friends.

"What's up Liah? You looking good as shit." He smiled wide as his eyes roamed up and down the length of my body.

I tried to play it cool, but my heart was racing hard as fuck. "What's going on? You look good too," I stated nervously.

"You must be clean 'cus I never seen a coke head glow up like you. Damn, that's what's up," he continued to marvel.

"Thanks. I um, I really have to get to work." I gave him a nervous smile.

"Yes you do, because I haven't forgotten about that $400 you stole from me. I need that shit back, or it's gon' get real ugly for you." The smile left his face, and anger danced in his eyes.

Leslie wasn't cute at all. On top of being ugly, his mama named him Leslie. He had dark, splotchy skin and a huge beer belly. He was flirting with me one night about two years ago, and I ended up going home with him. I got high as hell, and I honestly don't even remember what the sex was like. I do remember waking up from a deep sleep to him snoring beside me. I also remember taking $400 from his pants' pocket and hauling ass. I could talk about all the people I'd stolen shit from for an hour and that still wouldn't be everybody. I didn't want any problems because I really was trying to change my life. I was really excited about moving though, and I didn't want to have to get my dad to pay the first month's rent for me.

"I just started working here, but I promise you, just give me a few weeks, and I'll have your money. I swear." My voice held a pleading tone.

Leslie looked me up and down with disdain. "Don't think I'm not coming back for it. I should beat your ass right here and now for the stunt that you pulled, but fuck it. I want my money." He tossed me a hateful look before walking off towards his car.

I let out a shaky breath as I rushed to clock in. I could try and change my life all I wanted to, but I'd done too much dirt to ever be able to escape my past.

# 18

# JAYDA

"Well hi." I looked up at Azaan in surprise as he walked into his apartment with his son in tow. I recognized him from the pictures, and he was Azaan's twin.

I knew Azaan was coming back in town so I stopped by to cook for him and bring his mail from the club. He'd given me a key the day we made it official.

"What's up?" Azaan's face held a hint of frustration. He looked down at his son. "Tell Ms. Jayda hello."

"Hi." His son smiled bashfully.

"Hi handsome. He's so cute," I gushed.

Azaan got him comfortable on the couch and found some cartoons on the television. He then pulled me into the kitchen. "Vickie is getting her own crib, but it won't be ready for three days. I'm keeping him with me until her place is ready because I put her the fuck out of mine. I hate to bother you, I swear I do, but I can't go to the club with him. Do you mind running it for a few more days?"

I could tell from his eyes and his facial expression that Azaan was stressed out to the max. I tried to wrap my mind around everything that he was saying. "Sure. I don't mind helping at the club, but I don't mind watching him either if you want to go by the club. What happened?"

Instead of answering my question, Azaan walked over to me and invaded my personal space. He placed his hands on my ass, covered my lips with his, and eased his tongue in my mouth. He kissed me so passionately and sensually that my pussy started throbbing, and I had to remember that his son was in the other room. He finally stopped kissing me and took a step back. "I'm real close to murdering that bitch," he stated through clenched teeth.

I raised my eyebrows. "I enjoyed the hell out of that kiss, but can you tell me what happened?"

"I popped up at the crib and caught her in the bed I bought, in the house that I paid for with another nigga. Jayda, only God kept me from putting a bullet in her head."

My eyes widened in shock. That shit was crazy as hell, and I could tell from the look on his face that he was dead serious about wanting to kill her. "Wow. Damn." I wasn't sure what else to say.

"I beat that nigga's ass and put both of them out my shit. When she's settled in her own crib, and I'm positive my son is living in acceptable conditions, then I'll take him back. She ain't shit, but she's a good mom. As much as I hate her right now, I won't even do her like that. Even though I want to. Plus, my son loves his mother."

"Wow, that's a lot." I stared at Azaan. I couldn't even lie. The thought had crossed my mind that he may be in Miami messing around with his child's mother, but I didn't allow myself to be consumed by it. As usual, I kept myself busy and brushed off my insecurities when I didn't hear from Azaan often while he was away. Now, I knew why he'd been distant.

"I'm sorry you had to go through that," I stated in a low voice. "I cooked though. You think he's hungry? I can fix him a plate."

Azaan gave me a half-smile. "I appreciate that. I'm tired as fuck. If you can fix both our plates, after I eat, I'm going to bathe him and get him in bed. I want to stop by the club for about three hours if you don't mind staying with him. Then I'll come right back."

"Of course I don't mind."

I fixed all of us plates, and I couldn't stop smiling at the way Azaan doted on his son. He fed him, talked to him the entire time he bathed him, read him a story, and then got him settled on the huge leather couch with blankets and pillows. Azaan told him they'd go shopping tomorrow and get him a bedroom set. He also told him he could watch TV for one more hour, then he had to go to sleep.

Azaan hugged me on the way out the door, and I could look in his eyes and tell that he was exhausted. "Hurry back," I said before placing a kiss on his lips. "I wish you wouldn't even go."

"I won't be gone long," he was so tired he mumbled the words.

I cuddled up on the couch with Aheem hoping that I wouldn't have to beat the brakes off his mother in the near future. I no longer had to be worried about Azaan taking her back, but that didn't mean that she would give him up so easily. His son spoke very well to only be two, and I could tell he was smart. He asked me a few questions. He even asked me for a snack. I gave him some cookies and milk, then he climbed in my lap and went to sleep. He was the sweetest little boy, and for the first time in a while, I thought about the child that I lost.

I dozed off too and woke up to Azaan walking in the front door. Aheem was still laying on me. I looked at the cable box and saw that it was a little after midnight. Azaan eased his son out of my lap and carried him in the back. I figured it would be awkward to have his son in the bed with a woman that wasn't his mother, so I was prepared to go home. I waited for Azaan to come back in the living room.

"Thank you. I'm about to take a shower."

"Okay. I'm going to head home so you and baby boy can have the bed."

Azaan's eyebrows dipped low. "Nah, don't go home. We can sleep on the couch or make a pallet on the floor. I'm trying to sleep with you tonight." He was almost pouting.

I smiled. "Okay. Go take a shower."

I had clothes at Azaan's place, so I changed into something to sleep in. While Azaan was in the shower, I pulled one of his thick comforters from the closet and laid it out on the living room floor. I'd rather sleep on the floor than a couch and be cramped up. I then got a blanket and two pillows. The comforter was so thick that I couldn't even tell I was on the floor. By the time Azaan got out of the shower, I was comfortable and scrolling through my phone. He got behind me and wrapped his arm around my waist. He let out a content sigh, and I knew he was happy to finally be able to lie down.

He placed a kiss on my shoulder and five minutes later, he was snoring in my ear. I smiled and snuggled up against him. It didn't take long for sleep to take over me, but soon, I was aroused from my sleep. I felt Azaan's hard dick poking me in the butt, and his lips were placing soft kisses along the nape of my neck. He'd gotten a little bit of rest, and now he was ready to get some. I turned over and we stared at each for a brief second before I made my way to his crotch to give him some good head. My man was home, and I was about to fuck him right back to sleep.

# 19

# DIOR

"How are you doing boo?" one of my cast mates, Alanda, stood up and hugged me. The cameras were rolling, and we were shooting this scene in a restaurant. It was my first outing with the girls since my "miscarriage." Of course, I didn't really lose the baby so there was no footage of me at the hospital. Just me at home resting and Marshon taking care of me.

"I'm good. Thank you for asking." I sat down at the table and the waitress came over to take my order.

"How are you holding up?" Carmen, the bitch I didn't like, asked. She always had a shit eating smirk on her face that always made it seem as if she was up to something or not being genuine. I knew she didn't give a damn about how I was doing.

Carmen's man had money, and her father was a retired NBA player, so that hoe had old money. She was dressed in a bright yellow maxi dress that looked so pretty against her dark skin. Her hair was slicked back into a long ponytail that touched her ass damn near, and her ears, wrist, and neck were draped in diamonds. Her face was beat to perfection, and the potent scent of her expensive perfume filled the air and almost overpowered the smell of the food. Her yellow Chanel bag sat atop the table for all to see.

"I'm good. It was very early in the pregnancy, so I hadn't really had time to process the fact that I was even having a baby. Everything just happened so fast."

Carmen picked up her glass of wine and took a sip. "Hmmm, interesting."

I frowned up my face. "What do you mean interesting? Is there something you want to say?" That bitch thought she was the queen B. She started the most shit and had been in the most fights out of everyone in the group. She had a two-year-old son and spent damn near all of her air time being messy. She really irked my nerves. If she thought I was going to bite my tongue or kiss her ass, then she thought wrong.

"I mean *your* friend stated that you may not have had a miscarriage. So, were you really pregnant? Did you get an abortion?"

As warm as my face grew from the anger soaring through my body, I knew my face had to be red. "Fuck you mean my friend?" I looked around the table in bewilderment. All of the ladies had looks on their faces like they knew a secret. I was the only one out of the loop. I looked back over at Carmen. "Why don't you fill me in since you're always starting shit."

She jerked her neck back and let out a chuckle. "I'm always starting shit? Nah, I just don't mind calling people on their bullshit. During my charity event, your little friend Nico had too much to drink, and he simply insinuated that you may not have had a miscarriage."

I couldn't believe that bumpy dick bastard. It was because of me that he'd been given airtime twice on the show, and that's how he did me in my absence? Carmen had to just be starting shit. She had to be. Since I hadn't actually heard what Nico said, I tried not to jump to conclusions, but I was pissed. "Well it's a good thing that Nico isn't in my vagina nor my personal business. As far as if I was really pregnant, Kylie was there when I took the test. I don't have to lie about that shit."

Carmen held her hands up in surrender. "Don't shoot the messenger babe. That's your friend, and I just think you should watch him."

"Fuck this," I spat, scooting my chair back. In trying to convince Carmen that I wasn't lying about being pregnant, it hit me that Fahan may actually see the shit. Even if I tried to tell him the pregnancy was fake, I was going hard trying to convince Carmen that it wasn't. I just wanted my life back. Everything I said on camera had the potential to be used against me, and I was over it.

I snatched my purse up and headed for the exit. As I suspected, Kylie followed after me. "Why are you leaving?" She felt like everyone was supposed to run towards drama for this bullshit ass show, and I was tired. The shit was going to end up costing me my man if I didn't get a handle on things. I already told him that I couldn't marry him and pissed him off.

"Because I don't feel like doing this shit with Carmen today. Her lying ass," I hissed. "What will she gain from starting shit between me and my friend?"

Kylie sighed. "I went over the footage from the event, and he did say something to that effect. Amber asked how you were doing after the miscarriage and he mumbled under his breath, *believe she had a miscarriage if you want to.* Nobody coaxed him to say that. He said it on his own. In his defense, he was very drunk, but it makes me question if he's your friend for real."

Nico brought his fat ass in the apartment after the charity event coming in my room being fake as fuck talking about Carmen's dress and her hair. Not once did he mention that he threw me under the bus. I couldn't wait to get home. I was so mad that tears sprang to my eyes. I just wanted to go home. I just wanted this show shit to be over. Kylie pulled me into her arms for a hug.

"I can't tell you not to be hurt because you were betrayed by someone that you looked out for. It's not much but Nico will get $500 for each time he appeared on the show, and he was on the show because of you. Tomorrow is the last day of filming before we wrap everything up to be edited. The reunion is next weekend, and then you'll be done with us for two months. It's supposed to be a secret, but the head producer loves you and Marshon and she wants the both of you back for season two. There will be more pay and more episodes."

I swiped my tears away angrily. "I'm done with this shit. I don't want to come back for season two."

Kylie didn't pay any attention to what I said. "Come back inside and let Carmen know that you did miscarry. Tell her to mind her business and that Nico is a fraud. You can do it. Don't run away."

I was so ready to be done with those bitches it wasn't even funny. Instead of leaving, I went back inside though, but I was still furious. If Carmen said one wrong word to me, I was gon' rock her shit. I couldn't wait to get home and go off on Nico. I was so anxious to get at his ass that my hands were shaking.

* * *

FOUR HOURS LATER, I pulled up in front of my apartment and hopped out of my car. I slammed the door shut and stuck my key in the door hard as hell. As soon as I entered the apartment, I heard Nico's loud ass, dramatic voice coming from his bedroom. I stomped in the direction of his room with pure hatred in my heart. I'd witnessed him be messy plenty of times, but I never thought he'd direct his messiness at me. When I barged in his room, he was laid on his back in some booty shorts and a too tight tee shirt. He was talking to some nigga on Facetime.

"You a disloyal ass bitch," I barked, and he looked up at me like a deer that had been caught in headlights.

"Excuse me?" he screeched and sat up on the bed. He knew I was about to dig into his ass, so he looked at the phone screen. "Let me call you back," he stated with an attitude and ended the call.

"Nigga, you said on camera that I didn't have a miscarriage?! You really said that shit. Carmen brought that shit up today, and I almost knocked the spit out her mouth. You foul as hell for that. You begged to be on the show, so you could do me wrong?" I yelled. I was angry and hurt which was a deadly combination.

The fact that Nico didn't immediately deny the shit told me everything I needed to know. Carmen didn't lie and neither did Kylie. Nico sat there trying to recall what he said or either trying to come up with a lie. "When did I say that?" He had the nerve to look confused.

"Nigga you know when you said it! When were you around them? It's all good though 'cus you 'bout to get the fuck out my shit. Now." I headed for the closet and yanked it open. I started pulling Nico's clothes off the rack and tossing them on the floor.

I was mad, but I wasn't dumb. He might be feminine, but he was still a man. A man that outweighed me, so I knew I couldn't beat his ass. He was getting up out of my apartment though, and I put that on everything. Fake ass nigga.

Nico hopped up off the bed. "Are you serious right now Dior? I don't remember half of what I said that night. The champagne was free, and I was drunk as shit. I can fix it," he stated in a panic.

"Nah, you can't fix shit." I continued yanking his clothes off the rack and tossing them on the floor. "You wouldn't have to fix it had you never said it. That was the fakest shit you could have ever done. I've been nothing but a friend to you and that's how you repay me? You know that shit is going to be on TV, and you know Fahan is going to see that shit. How could you? You got to go. Tonight."

Nico's broke ass didn't even have a lot of clothes, so I was done in less than ten minutes. He worked hard, and he claimed he got so much money out of niggas, but he didn't have shit to show for it. He'd spend $200 on one outfit and wear that bitch over and over until I was tired of looking at it. I was tired and out of breath after yanking all his shit off the hangers. My chest heaved up and down as I watched him collect his shit off the floor.

"You can't make me get out tonight. I've already paid my half of the rent for next month. You can't put me out without notice."

"The fuck I can't. Your name isn't on the lease. I was doing you a favor, and now since you're disrespectful and flaw, that shit is a wrap."

"Don't act like I wasn't helping you too. Don't act like Azaan been giving you money from day one. That little money that Fahan sends you isn't enough to put a dent in your bills. Don't think because you're on this fake ass show, you can switch up. Bitch, I didn't even spill no real tea, but I could." He smirked.

"And I can spill it too, you fuckin' herpes monster. Bumpy dick bitch. Get out! I don't care what you paid. I'll give that shit back, but you getting out."

"Girl, fuck you and this apartment." Nico spun on his heels and started packing his shit.

The doorbell rang, and I hoped it was one of my neighbors complaining about the yelling. I was gon' curse their ass out too. Nico was getting the hell up out of my crib, I didn't care if we had to call the police. I snatched the door open with an attitude, and the person I saw standing on my doorstep damn near made me faint. "Fahan?" I asked in a weak voice as my heart pounded in my chest.

"Fuck in here doing all that yelling?" he asked with a frown on his face.

## 20

# FAHAN

"F-Fahan what are you doing here?" Dior looked as if she'd seen a ghost. I had heard mad yelling when I walked up to her door, and all I wanted to know was what was going on. I hated to have to bust some ass hours after I got out of prison, but depending on what was going on inside, I would.

I stepped inside of the apartment without being invited. "Who you in here arguing with Dior?" I looked around and didn't see anybody in the living room.

My girl was looking like she was about to faint, and the thought of her being in there with another man crossed my mind. Just as I was about to go looking through the apartment myself, she spoke up.

"I was talking to Nico. We had a fight, and I told him he had to get out."

I wasn't sure what was up with Dior and why she was looking so scared all of a sudden. I knew she lived with the dude Nico, and that didn't bother me. After all, he was gay. It's not like she would fuck him, and she told me that he would be out by the time I came home. I didn't mind him being there as long as he didn't bother me. I was aware that I popped up early so I wasn't going to demand that he get out, but it seemed as though the job had been done for me. Nico came twisting out of the room with a scowl on his face rolling a suitcase behind him. Like Dior, he looked stunned when he saw me. I was really curious as to what their argument was about. Dior had told me a few times that he was a dramatic and flamboyant type of nigga but from what I knew, they got along well. She'd never told me about them fighting before.

Nico headed for the front door. "I'll get the rest of my things tomorrow."

I leaned against the wall and eyed Dior. "What's going on?"

"He's just annoying and he gossips like a bitch. I wasn't in the mood for him today and I spazzed. But what are you doing here Fahan?"

I ignored the fact that she tried to make light of the situation with Nico. The way I heard her ass yelling told me that she was pissed. Now, she wanted to act all calm, but I knew better. I decided to let it go, because she looked good as fuck. Dior was gorgeous natural, but she had a face full of make-up, and she damn near looked like a different person. I could tell that she'd been filming for the show. She had on some jeans that hugged her frame like a second skin. She was damn near busting out of them joints and seeing as how I hadn't had pussy in a year, my dick was hard just from her stance. When I thought about it, I didn't care about Nico and their petty ass argument. I was in the apartment with my baby, and I could get some pussy. I silently prayed that her period wasn't on.

"It seems that my brother greased the palms of the right people. He broke bread with a few people, and here I am in the flesh. You happy to see a nigga?"

"Of course I'm happy to see you. I'm still in shock that you're even standing here. Oh my god baby, I missed you." Dior came over to me and wrapped her arms around my neck.

"That's what I'm talking about," I stated before inhaling her scent. A nigga was free, and I was happy as fuck. Azaan had picked me up earlier with mad clothes and shoes in the car for me. He then took me to get something to eat and took me by the club. I was full as a tick and ready for some pussy. "You got some weed in here?" I questioned.

Dior took a step back. "No, but I can get you some. I'm going to call this girl I know; her dude sells weed. There's some henny in the kitchen. We gon' get right. I'm 'bout to run you a bath." Dior was more than ready to cater to a nigga, and I didn't have any objections.

My eyes roamed over her slim thick frame. "Do that shit. I'm ready to slide up in them guts."

Dior smiled and pulled her cell phone from her back pocket. She moved in the apartment after I went away, so I took the time to walk around and see what it looked like. It was nice, and it would most definitely do until I made the money to move us into a bigger crib. After I gave myself a tour, I went out to the car that Azaan was letting me use, and I grabbed my bags of clothes from the back seat. I had thanked him multiple times for having the damn good sense to reach out to the right people and get me out of prison. I hadn't even told him or Dior about my book deal, but I would soon enough. I had a year-long vacation. I was ready to chill for the night and get some pussy but after that, I was going to be ready to work. I'd missed my girl, but I wasn't about to spend days cupcaking. I was going to take advantage of the time that Azaan was in town and learn everything there was to know about running the club. I said a silent prayer and thanked God for the fact that I didn't have to come home to the streets.

I was a little mad at God after my mom died, but I was over it. When I sat back and looked at shit, I was blessed. We all had to go sometime, and it was just my mom's time to go. Azaan had stepped up to the plate and done more for me than he had to do, and I was extremely grateful. I took my bags in the bedroom, and Dior followed me.

"He said he can pull up in ten minutes. You hungry? I haven't cooked but I can whip something up."

"Nah, I'm good. Azaan took me to a banging ass soul food spot. I just want to wash my ass right now. What I want to eat can't be put on a plate, you heard me?"

Dior blushed. "Well let me go run you a bath. Hold on."

I pulled some boxer briefs and some pajamas from the bag. Azaan had gotten me everything from a toothbrush to deodorant. I was happier than I had been in a very long time. Dior got my bath water started and a few seconds later, she came in the room carrying a glass, and I knew she had fixed me some henny. "Hopefully by the time you come out of the bathroom, I'll have the blunt rolled. Did Azaan get you a phone? If not, I'll add another line to my plan tomorrow."

I could tell that my baby was happy to see me. "Yeah, he did. That nigga thought of everything." I glanced at her finger. I knew what she told me about the show, but it still made me feel some type of way that she didn't have the ring on that Azaan had gotten her on my behalf. "So you don't wear your ring huh?" I asked before taking a sip of the potent drink in my hand.

Dior glanced down at her hands. "I just don't wear it when I'm filming, but tomorrow is my last episode. After that, I'm never taking it off. I already told you I'm not doing season two. I want to go ahead and start planning our wedding."

I was glad that Dior had decided on her own not to keep going with the show. Now that I was home, I for damn sure wasn't about to be hiding and pretending like she wasn't my girl. Fuck all that shit. The show may have been offering her money per episode, but she'd never be broke as long as I was free. Even though we had the club, I was aware that Azaan was still doing his thing with pills. He made it clear that he didn't want me involved, and I didn't object. I wasn't trying to be greedy. As long as the club brought in enough money to pay the bills every month, then my hustling days were over. I only had to smell shit one time to know that it stunk.

I took my drink and headed for the bathroom. A nigga hadn't taken a tub bath since I was a kid, but after being in a filthy prison, I needed one. After taking my clothes off, I eased down into the warm water. I looked around the bathroom proud of my girl and what she accomplished. Even if she did have a roommate, when shit got thick and I left, she was able to hold her own. She didn't have to run home to her mom or fuck with niggas just to keep the bills paid. Shorty worked her ass off and held shit down. That was admirable in my eyes for sure.

By the time my glass was empty, I had a slight buzz. I drained the water from the tub, stood up, took a shower and washed off. After I was done, I wrapped a towel around my waist and headed into the bedroom. Dior was sitting on the edge of the bed rolling a blunt, and my dick got hard. I watched her as she sparked the blunt and hit it three times before passing it to me.

"I'm going to fix you another drink. By the time I get out of the shower, you're gonna be good and fucked up." She gave me a sexy grin.

I puffed on the blunt and held the weed smoke in my lungs for a minute. That shit was potent as hell, and I broke out into a coughing fit. I swear I only hit the blunt four times, and I was high as a kite. Dior brought me drink number two, and I sat back and sipped and chilled while she took a shower. I pulled the phone that Azaan got me from my pocket and tried to figure out how to work the shit. I'd only been gone a year but he'd bought me a much newer phone than I had before I went away. I became lost in the technology and before I knew it, the bathroom door was opening. A floral fragrance filled my nostrils, and I looked up.

"Damn," I mumbled. Dior was walking towards me naked as hell. I put the blunt on the ashtray on her nightstand and drained the rest of the liquor from my glass. Dior stepped in between my legs and pulled my towel from around my waist.

"I missed you so much," she stated in a low voice before dropping down and taking my dick into her mouth. I would be the first to admit my dick wasn't the biggest in the world, but I'd never hit a chick that didn't fall in love with the shit.

"I missed you too," I confessed as my dick hit the back of her tonsils.

I knew I was going to nut fast as hell off the head, and that was fine. By the time I started digging in Dior's pussy, I wanted to be able to last for a while. I was sure with the help of the liquor I would. I moaned as her head bobbed up and down on my dick and she coated my shaft with her spit. Dior stared into my eyes, and I knew I wouldn't be able to last much longer.

"Suck that shit," I coached her.

Dior sped up the pace and that familiar sensation brewing in my nut sack had my toes curling. Her wet ass mouth was giving off crazy sound effects and turning me on at the same time. "Just like that," I urged as I grabbed a handful of her hair. "Fuuuckkkk," I groaned as nut shot through my dick and into Dior's mouth.

She kept sucking for a minute, and a nigga had to pull his lips in to keep from sounding like a bitch. She maintained eye contact as she swallowed my nut up. I stood up ready to do some damage. Dior and I switched positions and it was me in between her legs. From the moment my mouth covered her swollen clit, she whimpered in ecstasy. My tongue swirled around her love button, and she got loud as hell when I slid a finger into her slit while sucking on her peach.

"Babbbyy," she moaned as she gyrated and fucked my face with her pussy.

Her juices slid down the crack of her ass, and I tried to get every bit. When my tongue swiped her ass, Dior's moans got louder and more erotic. My dick got right back hard, and I couldn't wait to slide up inside her, but I wanted her to cum first. I sucked harder and faster, and Dior's ass lifted off the bed and she screamed as she creamed into my mouth.

"Ummmmm." I ate that shit up like it was the best thing I'd ever tasted. Once I had devoured every drop, I moved up and placed the head of my dick in Dior's pussy. Fuck, that shit felt good. I slowly eased my way in as if I was trying to savor the moment.

Dior moaned and opened her legs wider as I leaned in to kiss her. I had a year and some change worth of fucking to catch up on, so I hoped her ass was ready to go all night.

* * *

"Nigga what the fucckkkkk." I looked at Azaan with my mouth hanging open as he told me everything that went down with him and Vickie. I couldn't believe what he was telling me. Vickie acted like she loved the ground Azaan's ass walked on and maybe she did, but she for sure messed up by getting caught up with Meer and not putting Azaan up on game.

He shook his head. "Shit been crazy. I'm taking Aheem back to her tomorrow. I was supposed to take him back a few days ago, but I didn't feel like taking that drive. Plus, I been missing him and I wanted to spend some more time with him, so fuck what Vickie wanted. I want you to come by the crib later. Bring Dior, so you can meet my lady."

I chuckled. "Nigga you and Vickie just broke up and you got a lady already? You didn't want to be single and chill for a bit?"

Azaan laughed. "I thought about it for real. All these chicks in Charlotte are new to me, so I could have been like a kid in a candy store, but I chose not to go that route. Jayda is real cool. She mad different. Her vibe is on another level."

"Okay, okay, well I definitely need to meet her then. I'll shoot Dior a text and let her know what's up. What time you thinking?"

"Around five so we can be back here around the time the crowd starts to come in. I'm real happy with the way things have been going. Matter of fact, let's head in the office and look at the numbers from the first week in business."

I followed behind Azaan eagerly. I was ready to learn. Now that he had a girl in Charlotte, I wasn't sure when he was going back to Miami to live, but I wanted to hold my weight when it came to the club. He got it off the ground while I was doing my bid, so now I had to come home and do my part. When he left to take my nephew back to Miami, I wanted him to be comfortable that I had things under control.

We spent the next few hours going over everything. He also called all the staff in for a brief thirty-minute meeting that he told them to clock in for. It was so I could be introduced to everyone and the role they played at the club. I couldn't even front. The bartenders and bottle girls were all bad as fuck. I started to ask Azaan how he was able to work at the club and resist all that thick ass temptation, but I already knew the answer. Azaan was about his money, and he didn't shit where he ate. It's bad business to be the boss and be fucking your workers, but all of them were gorgeous as fuck. I loved Dior with everything in me, but I had to remind my dick at least three times that I was in a relationship.

Even one of the shorties that worked in the kitchen caught my eye. Shorty was too damn fine to be working in a kitchen, and that was just my opinion. She looked kind of quiet and reserved so maybe that's why she chose to work in the kitchen and not be a bartender or a cocktail waitress. I couldn't knock the way she chose to get her money. I found out through introductions that her name was Liah. She was the only one working in the kitchen that wasn't a middle-aged woman. She looked out of place among them, but again, if she didn't mind working in the kitchen, that's what it was. The bartenders and cocktail waitresses were all gorgeous in a bad bitch type of way. Even off the clock, the majority of them had on long, dramatic lashes, super long, bright, crazy shaped nails, and all that extra shit. Liah was dressed casually in some jeans, a white tank top, and some Vans. Her hair was in a bob, and she didn't have on any make-up, and she still stood out to me. I could appreciate females that cared about their appearance and went all out to look good if that's what they liked, but I could appreciate simple beauty as well. Liah didn't have on any jewelry, not even a watch, and her nails weren't done, but I still found myself glancing in her direction several times.

Her sun kissed skin was smooth and pretty, and she was the perfect size. Once the meeting was over, I started to ask Azaan what her deal was, but I decided against it. I was with Dior, and I didn't need to be interested in the back story on any of my female employees. After we were done at the club, I headed home to take a shower and get ready to go to Azaan's crib and meet this girl of his. Plus, I'd never met my nephew in person, and I was excited about that. With Azaan being his dad, I knew he was spoiled, but I wanted to stop by the store and get Dior to help me pick out a few toys for him from his uncle Fahan.

When I walked in the apartment, Dior was dressed in a pair of tight, light denim jeans that fit like a glove at the top and flared out at the bottom like bell bottoms they used to wear back in the day. She had on a fitted pink tank top and some pink sandals. I smiled when I saw the rock Azaan got her for me sitting nice and pretty on her finger. I walked up behind her and kissed her on the back of the neck. "You look nice."

Dior smiled as she smoothed lip gloss across her lips. "Thank you baby."

I headed to take a shower and get dressed and then we headed for Target to get Aheem some toys. When we pulled up at Azaan's crib, I admired the neighborhood and the G wagon in the driveway with North Carolina tags. "Oh okay, his girl must have some paper." I nodded in approval.

"So he not with Vickie no more at all or does he just have a side chick in North Carolina?" Dior asked with her face frowned up.

I chuckled. "Fix ya face. That man ain't cheating. He and Vickie are done."

She looked shocked. "Really? What happened?"

I loved Dior and I rocked with her, but no way was I telling her the whole shit with Meer. It was too messy. I had spoken to my aunt since I'd been home, and she was a mess. She was sick with worry. Meer's remains still hadn't been found. It was like he vanished into thin air, and my aunt was on the verge of a mental breakdown. I loved her, but I was riding with Azaan on that one. Fuck Meer's pussy ass, and Vickie got what she deserved. Her loyalty should have been to her man and the father of her son.

I shrugged one shoulder passively. "She was lying and being sneaky, and Azaan wasn't going for that shit."

"Lying and sneaky how?"

I kissed my teeth and smiled. "Nigga, get yo' nosey ass out the car. None of that is important. She had a good nigga, and she messed it up. Now he has a new broad. Let's go meet her."

I walked up to the door with Dior right on my heels. Shortly after I rang the bell, Azaan answered with Aheem on his hip. "Dang, look at my nephew looking just like his daddy," I admired. I'd seen plenty of pictures, but the shit was crazy in person how he really looked like a miniature Azaan.

"I know right. Say what's up Uncle Fahan," Azaan coached his son.

He smiled at me and repeated the words, and that made me smile. "What up lil' man? I brought you gifts."

Aheem's face lit up, and Azaan put him down so he could see what I got for him. Azaan and Dior spoke to one another and a pretty ass female entered the living room. Looking at her, I could see why my brother was digging her. Her smile was bright. "Hello, you must be Fahan and Dior. I'm Jayda, and the food is done."

"Hey, how you doing?" I spoke and then Dior did.

I pulled Aheem's gifts from the bags and Azaan told him he could play with his toys once we were done with dinner. I washed my hands and went into the kitchen where Jayda had set out steaming dishes of baked spaghetti, salad, corn on the cob, and breadsticks. Everything looked delicious, and for the past few days I'd been ecstatic not having to eat food that was prepared in the microwave.

Dior and Jayda hit it off well, and the two conversed about everything from the reality show to make-up and movies. Dinner with my brother was love, and I was eager to spend some more time with my nephew and then to hit the club. I was blessed that I came home to the life that I did, and I was determined to go super hard to show my appreciation for all that I'd been given. My main priorities were making Azaan and Dior proud and to also make them not regret holding me down and believing in me.

# LIAH

"Jayda, you really don't have to keep buying me stuff," I stated as I looked down at the huge box in her hands. "Really, you've done enough for me."

Just two days before, Jayda had bought me some towels, wash rags, and some decorative items for my bathroom. Now she was coming in with stainless steel pots and pans that I was sure cost a grip.

"It's nothing. You know I'm addicted to shopping. I'll try to stop, but I can't make any promises. So it looks like everything is coming along nicely. How are you doing?"

She placed the pots and pans set on my living room floor. I was officially out of the hotel and in my own place, and now I had to figure out a way to get Leslie his money. I didn't want any problems with him, and I was willing to do whatever I had to do. I was lowkey glad that Azaan was out of town because his brother seemed cool, and I was going to ask him if I could work my days off.

My parents always found reasons to come by and see me or pop up at my job. I felt like they wanted to actually see me. Just by talking to them on the phone, they wouldn't be able to see if I had relapsed. I didn't mind. They weren't overbearing with it, and I knew they just wanted the best for me. I wanted the best for myself, and I wanted to hurry up and give Leslie his money. It would be too easy for me to get stressed out about what I owed him and decide to sniff my problems away or to pop a pill and give zero fucks. Being high made me numb. It would have me walking the streets knowing that I owed Leslie and not caring. Being numb was also a good way to play with my life. He wasn't really a street nigga like that. Leslie wasn't as ruthless as Azaan, but I didn't doubt he might beat my ass for the money that I owed him.

"I'm thinking about inviting Azaan to Sunday dinner to meet Mom and Dad," Jayda revealed.

I raised my eyebrows. "You really like him huh? I think that's a good idea. It's clear to see he makes you happy, and I think that alone will make Mom and Dad happy. You know they worry about both of us," I mumbled the last part. I'm sure I'd stressed them out way more than Jayda had, but I also knew that they didn't like seeing her sad all that time after Biggs died.

"Yeah, I know. I think it's just in parents' nature to worry, but I'm good. They don't have to worry about me. Even if Azaan and I don't work out for some reason, I've spent enough time sulking. I want to just enjoy life and have beautiful memories." Jayda was glowing, and I was so happy for her. I was scared to be happy for myself because I knew every day I woke up, there was a possibility that I might relapse, and I didn't want that for myself, but addiction was a hell of a disease.

Jayda helped me in the apartment until it was time to go to work. She then dropped me off. "Liah!" I grimaced as I reached the door, and someone called my name.

I turned around and saw Leslie walking towards me. "What's good?"

I didn't try to hide my annoyance. "It hasn't even been a week yet," I snapped.

"Easy Baby Girl." He smirked at me. "Calm down with the attitude because I was being nice by even giving you two weeks. I didn't have to give you shit. I just wanted to stop by as a friendly reminder that I want my shit."

"And you'll get it," I stated through clenched teeth.

"Everything good here?" I looked up and saw fine ass Fahan.

I hadn't even noticed him walking up, that's just how aggravated Leslie had me. "Yeah everything is fine." I tossed a fake smile his way and used his presence as a distraction. I turned and entered the club leaving Leslie outside because the club wasn't open, and he couldn't come in yet.

Fahan was right behind me. "You good? Is that guy bothering you?"

Azaan couldn't have told his brother that I tried to rob him. There was no way, because Fahan was entirely too nice to me. "No, he wasn't bothering me. Before I clock in, can I ask you a quick question? Would it be okay if I work my days off? I really need the money." I was sure I sounded desperate, and I didn't even care. I wanted to be rid of Leslie.

"I don't have a problem with it. Excuse me if I overstep my boundaries, but you're too pretty to be in the kitchen. You never thought about being a cocktail waitress or a bartender?"

Did I look this man in the face and admit that I was a recovering addict and his brother didn't want me around the cash? It already bothered me every time I caught Azaan glaring at me like he hated my guts. I didn't want Fahan looking at me like that too. He was always so nice and soft, and I welcomed that. Maybe if I just snuck and did the shit while Azaan was out of town, I could make the money that I needed to pay Leslie back and then never do it again.

"I wouldn't mind waitressing just for the next two nights. I'm really fine working in the kitchen. I just need some fast money, and dancing is out of the question," I joked and gave him a nervous smile.

He smiled back. God that man was sexy. I didn't usually like face tattoos, but he made even that look good.

"That's what it is then. For the next two nights you can be a cocktail waitress."

"Thank you."

*  *  *

I WASN'T REALLY nervous the next night because even though I was dressed kind of skimpy, it wasn't like I was naked. I was just a waitress in a night club that served drinks rather than just food. I made sure to put on some make-up, and I flirted and smiled at the customers. Finessing men was something I'd been doing for a long time. When I wasn't stealing or selling ass, when I was on drugs, I was using men to support my drug habit. The first two hours of me working, I had made $150 and I knew I'd be able to pay Leslie back for sure. I was almost sad that I would have to go back to the kitchen. Not that I didn't like being in the kitchen, but the money from waitressing was faster. That gave me the idea to apply for some local restaurants and bars to work the evening shift a few days a week. I could come home with money every day rather than having to wait for a paycheck. Or better yet, I might apply to be a cocktail waitress at some other clubs. I didn't have to stay at Azaan's club knowing that he hated me.

Sometimes I forgot that I was clean, and I was actually pretty again. When I was on drugs, I was used to people staring at me because I looked bad. Now, they stared at me because I was cute. Men tried to talk to me almost daily. It was something that I wasn't used to. Derrin and I were still conversing, and we were even talking about going out again soon. I had a lot of things to be happy about.

"Okay, you look cute all dressed up," Sahara, one of the other waitresses, complimented me.

"Thank you." I smiled as I headed to the bar to fulfill an order.

Fahan was at the bar, and when he saw me, I saw the lustful look in his eyes. "You look nice. You sure you trying to go back in that kitchen? You can make some good ass money out here."

I swear I didn't want Azaan to tell Fahan the real reason why I was in the kitchen. I just prayed that if I acted like I was cool in the kitchen, that he'd drop it. "I'm sure. I actually like being in the kitchen."

My feet were killing me by the time I got off work, but I wasn't even going to complain. I had made $300 in tips. The next night I was going to only need $100 to pay Leslie his money, and anything I made after that, I could keep. It would be extra money in my pocket until I got paid. Yeah, maybe I'd go apply at another club after all.

## 2 2

# DIOR

"Dior and Marshon are a couple that fought hard this season, but they made up harder. Here's a look back at some of their most passionate moments." The host for the reality show reunion introduced Marshon and I, and I watched the TV prompters to see what footage was going to play.

We'd been filming the reunion for thirty minutes, and so far, two fights had broken out. Since the show hadn't aired yet, whatever footage they played at the reunion was the only footage that any of us had seen. We were seeing all the shady ass green screen moments with bitches talking shit and the edited scenes that would be displayed on TV, and my ass was sweating bullets.

I almost fainted when I saw cameras in the women's bathroom, and Kylie standing outside the stall asking me if I was okay. That sneaky ass got damn bitch. They had gotten shots of the pregnancy test. I wasn't even aware that she'd let the cameraman in the bathroom. My chest got tight and I felt as if I couldn't breathe. His sneaky ass was gone of course by the time I came out of the stall, but he went back in after I left and got a shot of the positive test. I wanted to run off that stage and break Kylie's fuckin' neck.

What I saw next really snatched my breath. It was me and Marshon in bed in the Airbnb. It was the night that I took the pill and we fucked for real. The camera crew wasn't there, but Marshon's bitch ass had set up his camera to record us fucking and the crew edited it to make it look like it was when we made up after he cheated on me. It was after we moved from the couch to the bed. Marshon and I were kissing hungrily as he moved in and out of me aggressively. The scene was hot and steamy and the crowd began to ouuuuuu and make all kinds of noise. There was no way on God's green Earth that I'd be able to convince Fahan that shit was fake. Marshon's bitch ass set me up.

I had to remind myself that I was under contractual obligation and after all I'd been through, I wanted my money. I would have to come up with a super good ass lie, well several super good ass lies, to save my ass with Fahan. I wanted to cry, I wanted to scream, I wanted to fuck some shit up, but I couldn't. Instead, I kept the act up.

"Dior, you and Marshon went through a lot this season, especially with the miscarriage. What's the status of your relationship now?"

"There is none," I stated calmly, and Marshon whipped his head in my direction. "I just decided that I don't want to be with him anymore," I stated passively, trying to keep my voice even.

The audience gasped, but I no longer gave a fuck about this fake ass storyline. Niggas were trying to ruin my life. "Marshon, did you know this?" the host asked him.

"Nah. I was under the impression that we were trying to make things work."

"Dior, what made you decide that you don't want to be with him anymore?"

"I just don't."

"Does your ex that's incarcerated have anything to do with that?"

"Maybe," I answered with hella attitude.

"When is he being released? Are you still in contact with him?"

"He's not on this show, therefore, I'm not talking about him. Marshon was cool, but I don't want to be with him anymore. There wasn't any real connection. I tried, it's a wrap." I hoped his bitch ass was mad at the way I was carrying him. That's what he got for taping us fucking. Cruddy ass nigga.

"Well you had a friend that appeared on the show, and it seems that he may have insinuated that you really didn't have a miscarriage," the host continued, and I lost my cool.

"Look, I'm not answering any more questions. Get me off this fuck ass shit," I snapped and stood up. I reached around myself and snatched the microphone off of me. I stormed towards the dressing room and locked my door. Kylie and other producers were knocking trying to get me to open up, but they could eat a dick.

Tears streamed down my face ruining my make-up as I took off the long sequined gown that I had on. I would have to go home and come up with a hell of a story to tell Fahan and pray to God that he didn't leave me once the show finally aired.

# 23

## AZAAN

"**W**hat's going on? Everything good?" I asked Fahan as I entered the office at the club. I stayed in Miami for two days making sure my son was good, and now I was back at work happy to be kicking it with my brother like old times.

"Everything has been love. You didn't have any problems with Vickie?" he inquired.

I kissed my teeth. "She did the usual crying and begging, but I'm not thinking about that shit she talking about. It's a wrap with us and it will be forever. Shit been going smooth here though?"

"Hell yeah. Last night we were packed to capacity. Aye bruh, you did the damn thing picking those strippers. I had to stop myself from throwing hella ones last night." Fahan laughed. "The temptation is too real, and every last one of them be flirting with a nigga. How do you do it?"

"Simple. As soon as I fuck a broad and she gets in her feelings, then shit will be bad for business. I don't know if it's 'cus we're new or because we have some of the baddest strippers in the city, but the club does very well. I don't want anything getting in the way of that, so I just keep in mind that I have a bad chick at home."

Fahan nodded in agreeance. "I feel you, but got damn. And it's not even just the strippers. Lil' mama that works in the kitchen is bad as hell too. I can't figure out for the life of me why she wants to work in the kitchen. Her nights off I let her work as a cocktail waitress, and she did damn good. I'm trying to get her to come out of the kitchen."

My jaw muscles tightened. There was only one pretty female that worked in the kitchen, so he had to be talking about Liah. So, that bitch came out of the kitchen and worked as a waitress while I was out of town. "You talking about Liah?" I asked for clarification as my nostrils flared.

Fahan could see that I was pissed. "Yeah, what's wrong? That's you or something?"

I frowned up my face. "Hell nah that ain't me. That's Jayda's sister, and Jayda is the only reason why Liah isn't floating in a river. That bitch basically blackmailed me into giving her a job. The bitch is a recovering fiend that used to cop from me. When I found out she was Jayda's sister, I cut her off. Told niggas not to serve her, so she got the bright idea to try and rob my trap with two of her friends. She drove the getaway car, and her friends are no longer breathing. I shot her ass in the head, but the bitch didn't die. That bitch stays in the kitchen, or she doesn't have a job," I growled.

My office door wasn't all the way closed, and my eyes shot up when it swung open. My heart rate increased when I saw Jayda standing there looking hurt. "Excuse me? What did you just say?"

Fuucckk. What a fine time to be reckless. I had said what I said, and I couldn't back down. She heard me anyway. There was a difference between withholding information and lying. I wasn't about to lie to her face. I licked my lips and ran my hand over my hair.

"I was the one that shot your sister. She tried to rob my trap with two of her friends."

Jayda's head jerked back. "Nobody was going to tell me? Both of y'all just been looking in my face every day knowing the truth?"

"Tell you for what Jayda? She didn't tell you, so you thought I was gon' volunteer the information? It was nothing personal at all, but what your sister did was foul. I didn't even know who she was when I got up on the car, and by the time I saw her face my finger was already squeezing the trigger. She violated. The reason she hasn't said anything is because she knows she was wrong."

"And what if she had died, huh? You woulda been watching me grieve, acting fake concerned, knowing the entire time that you were the one that murdered her. But I'm supposed to trust you knowing that?"

"I'm not 'bout to sit up here and explain myself as far as what coulda happened and what I woulda done. Your sister was dead ass wrong. She violated, and I did what I did. I didn't confess it to you, nah I didn't, and maybe I'm fucked up for that, but I'm not sorry for what I did. The only reason I gave her a job was for you. If you can't forgive me for the shit, then fuck it. That's what it is then." I really cared about Jayda, and I wasn't trying to come off like a hard ass, but her sister was fucked up, and she knew it.

The girl had stolen from her parents and probably a lot of other people. She kept doing it because she kept getting away with it, but she attempted to cross the wrong one when she came for me. Jayda and her people gave Liah passes because she was family. I didn't love that bitch, and I wasn't excusing shit.

"Wow." Jayda turned and left the office, and I blew out an exasperated breath.

"Damn, that was intense," Fahan stated.

"Tell me about it. Since I lost my girl, I should fire the bitch," I growled.

Fahan shook his head. "You don't think people can change?"

I looked at him like he'd lost his mind. "You ever seen a head change?"

"Yeah. Remember Ms. Jenny that stayed up the street from us? She was down bad when her son and I were in middle school. By the time I graduated from high school, she'd been clean for years and had gotten a job as a substance abuse counselor."

I kissed my teeth. "Whatever. That story is one in a million, and I feel like once a bitch is that weak and grimy she'll be that way forever."

I was salty that the situation was now another reason for Jayda to pull away from me after we'd been doing so good. Maybe the shit just wasn't meant to be.

# 24

## JAYDA

"So no one cared to tell me that I'm sleeping with the nigga that shot you?" I asked as I barged into Liah's apartment after she opened the door for me.

Her mouth opened, but no words came out. I could tell she was stunned by what I'd just said. I wasn't even about to explain to her how I found out. All she needed to know was that I knew, and I was pissed. I couldn't even sleep last night.

"Um well, I—" Liah stammered over her words. "I really didn't see a point in telling you because I know he makes you happy. Jayda, what I did was fucked up, and you're going to automatically feel like no matter what I did he shouldn't have shot me, but the streets don't work like that. I violated. I tried to rob that man's trap. I knew what the consequences could be, and I was too high to care."

It was my turn to be shocked. I stared at my sister for a moment before I could find words. "You're making excuses for him Liah?"

"No, I'm not making excuses for him. I'm taking responsibility for my actions, and what I did was wrong. How many times have I stolen from people? Again, you may think death is too harsh a price to pay for stealing, but I was in the streets for years. Like, I lived in the streets. I knew what I could be getting myself into. Niggas don't care that I'm a female. All Azaan saw was a woman driving the getaway car for the men that tried to rob him, and he snapped."

I was completely and utterly blown away that she was taking all of the responsibility. She even seemed to be defending Azaan. Gun violence was how I lost Biggs, and I just hated it. Period. I felt like niggas were too quick to pull guns on other people and take their lives. People out here acting like God. Like they had the right to take life away, but I knew who Azaan was. Him being in the streets didn't bother me until I found out he shot my sister. Before that, I gave him a pass for the shit. I really didn't know what to say.

"Jayda, my life is an everyday struggle. I love how far I've come and even still, some days I wonder if I'm going to end right back out there. Being an addict is the hardest thing in the world. People try to judge and say it's a choice, but once you become addicted, it goes way deeper than it being a simple choice. I have to fight every day to keep my sobriety. Some days the guilt of what I did to Mom and Dad alone make me sad, but all I can do is move forward. I can't harp on the past. I'm just glad that Azaan is the only one that seems to hate me. As long as you, Mom, and Dad forgave me, I'm good. He doesn't trust me, and honestly he shouldn't."

All of this was way too heavy for me. I really couldn't deal. I knew Azaan had told me that as soon as the club started doing well, he was going to be done with the streets. I worried about him so much because my heart wouldn't be able to take it if something happened to him the way it happened to Biggs. I should have tried harder to fight it months ago, but now it was as if I was stuck. I really liked Azaan, and the thought of ending our relationship made me sad. There was some shit I just couldn't keep going through. If I told him it was the streets or me, I wondered if he would really choose me. If he didn't, I'd feel real stupid. I took a deep breath and decided to stop making the whole thing about me for the moment. The person that Azaan shot wasn't even mad, but I was damn near going crazy over it.

"Of course we forgave you Liah, we love you. I know it has to be hard, but I hope you never forget that we're always here. If you need to start going to meetings or anything, I'll go with you. If you ever need to talk, if you ever feel the urge to use, I'm here. I'll stop whatever I'm doing to come to you. I'm so proud of you."

I meant every word that I said. Liah looked better than she had in many years. She hadn't been sober since she was in high school. She walked over to me, and we hugged. "It may sound weird, but don't let me be the deciding factor in whether or not you stay with Azaan. Okay?"

"Um, sure," I replied in a hesitant voice. I took a step back. "It must be hard for you working at the club though. It doesn't make you uncomfortable?"

Liah shrugged one shoulder. "Like I said, I understand why he hates me. I even kind of insinuated to him that if he didn't give me a job, you might find out that he shot me. I haven't exactly been an angel. He rarely comes in the kitchen though. I'm not even around him that often. Honestly, I have been thinking about applying at some other clubs to be a bottle girl. I like the money much better doing that compared to working in the kitchen."

I nodded. "Whatever you think is best for you, I'm with it."

"Thank you. I love you Jayda."

"I love you too Liah."

I left my sister's apartment feeling almost as confused as before I arrived. I was kind of shocked that she was urging me to be with Azaan after he shot her. Even if she was in the wrong. To see her take accountability for her actions, was a new Liah. One that I'd never seen before, and it dawned on me that my sister had come a very long way. In a fucked up way, if Azaan had never shot her, she would probably have never changed. I still didn't know what I was going to do about my situation with him. It seemed as if every time I tried to get comfortable with the fact that I was moving on and finally able to be in another relationship, something would occur to make me doubt that.

\* \* \*

*"I CAN'T DRINK BAE."*

*Biggs' eyebrows furrowed from confusion. His honey-colored eyes flickered with interest in what I would say next. "Why, what's wrong? You good?"*

*"Yeah, I'm good. So, I was going to surprise you on your birthday, but I'm pregnant. I took the test this morning."*

*Biggs' eyes widened. "You dead ass serious ma?" He looked like he wanted to lose his cool, but he was scared that I would tell him it was a joke.*

*I giggled. "I'm dead serious. I still have the test. It's at home though."*

*Biggs pushed his chair back, came over to where I was seated, leaned down, and planted peck after peck after peck on my lips. He must have kissed me thirty times. "I fuckin' love you." He peered into my eyes as if I was the only person on Earth that he ever had and ever would love.*

A tear spilled over my eyelid and trickled down my cheek as I thought back to that day in Atlanta almost five years ago. The day that I told Biggs I was pregnant with his child. I stood in my bathroom staring down at the pregnancy test in my hands. I had only been late once before, and that's when I was pregnant. My cycle was two days late when ordinarily it came like clockwork. Azaan and I had for sure been having a whole lot of sex. Like tons of sex, and we'd stopped using condoms, so me being pregnant wasn't a far-fetched idea at all. I was nervous to find out because we weren't exactly in a good place. Despite having talked to my sister earlier, I still needed some time and some space. Maybe a few days without seeing Azaan or talking to him would give me a clue as to what I should do. The nigga hadn't even reached out to me though, and that was making me feel some type of way. He was in the wrong, but he was acting as if he didn't give a damn if I was angry or not, and that was somewhat of a red flag for me.

Tired of standing in the bathroom, I inhaled a deep breath and opened the box. After pulling the test from the foil package, I pulled my jeans and panties down and peed on the stick. Once I was done, I put the cap back on it and placed the test on the counter. I took longer than usual to wipe myself, flush the toilet, and wash my hands. Once I was done, I stared at my reflection in the mirror. If I was pregnant, if I was carrying another child, this time my head had to be right. I couldn't help the fact that Biggs got killed and I grieved his death, but Azaan wasn't dead. No matter what was going on between us, I refused to stress myself to the point of possibly losing another baby. I didn't want to suffer through another miscarriage, and I for sure didn't want to terminate the pregnancy. Everyone didn't have that fairytale whirlwind romance and then marriage before they brought kids into the world.

If Azaan was nothing else, he was a damn good father. Despite what was going on with us, I couldn't find it in my heart to believe that he'd ever do my child dirty, and as long as he was there for the child, then I could find a way to be content. Mentally, I put my big girl panties on, and I looked down at the test. Two pink lines stared back up at me. I was carrying Azaan's child.

## 25

## FAHAN

I walked up behind Dior and wrapped my arms around her, and shorty jumped. I held onto her tightly and looked in the mirror at her reflection. "Why you been so jumpy and zoned out? What's good ma?" I asked, wondering if I'd done something wrong and pissed her off. She wasn't really acting mad though. More like nervous.

When I got in from work, she was asleep, but I woke her up by sliding dick in her. That morning, I woke up to her topping me off, and we had sex again. Since she didn't work anymore and filming was over, most days we spent time together after I woke up. Some days we went to breakfast, early movies, the mall, etc., and some days, we just chilled at the crib. I liked working at night and spending my days with Dior. It beat running the streets and having to worry about losing my freedom again.

Dior turned around to face me, and she could barely look me in the eyes. Shorty looked pale as fuck. "We need to talk." I knew from the way she was acting, it wasn't anything good, and that put me on the defensive.

I took a step back. "A'ight. Speak."

Dior shifted her weight from one leg to another. "Fahan, you know I love you more than anything and—"

"Don't even come at me like that ma." I kept my tone low, but there was no mistaking the seriousness that my voice held. "When somebody starts off with some bullshit like that, it just makes me feel like they're about to run game on me. Don't insult my intelligence, and don't take all day. Spit that shit out," I demanded. A nigga was anxious to know what had shorty looking like she'd seen a ghost.

Dior swallowed. Hard. "Ever since I fell out with Nico, he's been on some real bitch shit." Tears filled Dior's eyes, but I wasn't making one move to comfort her. Not until I knew what she had to tell me.

"The few times he was on the show went to his head, and now he's clout chasing. The storyline with Marshon and I got really intense. I faked a pregnancy and a miscarriage, but Nico is going around telling people that I had an abortion. He's saying that I had an abortion because when my real boyfriend got out of prison, I didn't want to have to tell him that I was pregnant. He photoshopped all these fake ass receipts, and they're floating around social media."

I pinched the bridge of my nose. I'd always had a quick temper, and I was trying so very hard to keep my composure. I didn't want to black out and do some shit that I might regret. Despite how heated I was, I was going to try and get all the information before I spazzed on Dior. I had one got damn request for that fuck ass reality show, and that was that she didn't go up there making me look stupid. From the way she was crying and acting all nervous, I was 'bout to be looking stupid. My phone started going off crazy, and I only looked at it to make sure Azaan wasn't trying to reach me. After pulling my phone from my pocket, I saw that I had damn near thirty Instagram notifications which didn't make any sense to me because I was barely on IG. I hadn't posted a picture in three days and that was at the club. I hadn't even been on social media at all since I woke up, so why were my notifications going crazy? Only way for me to find out was to look and see.

My blood began to boil as I read the first notification. Some gossip blog had tagged my name. Seems they did some digging and found out that I was Dior's incarcerated boo, as they called me. My picture was in a collage with Marshon and Dior. The caption went on to talk about how I was the person that Marshon got mad at Dior for going to visit. It even had what I was locked up for and talked about how I used to play ball in college. These muhfuckas were worse than the feds. That's why I didn't play with that social media shit like that because it could for real get somebody killed.

The next picture was of some text messages between Nico and Dior when she was telling him what time she scheduled the appointment for her abortion, and she asked if he could go with her. My nostrils flared, and I clenched my jaw muscles together so tight that shit hurt. I stared at the messages. Dior knew that I wasn't on social media heavy like that anymore, but I had the shit before I went away. I wasn't so stupid and green that I couldn't decipher between some photoshopped shit and some real legit text messages. The next slide consisted of text messages between the two of them when Nico was asking her if she really wanted to get rid of her baby, and she said she had to. This muhfucka had really played my face. I thought she was holding it down while I was away, but I was wrong as fuck.

All the other notifications were the same shit. Blogs saying that Dior was just using Marshon until I came home and all kinds of other shit. The rest of the notifications were from people following me and commenting on my pics. It bugged me out that I had gone from 1,100 followers to 4,000. That shit was crazy as hell. Females were commenting on my shit talking about how sexy I was. The thirst was real as fuck. All that could wait though. I had some business to attend to with Dior's trifling ass.

"These shits is fake huh?" I asked, glaring at her, daring her to lie.

Dior erupted into tears. "I swear on everything Fahan, that the whole time you were locked up, I only had sex one time. I swear on my mama." She cried hard as hell and snot poured from her nose. My blood boiled upon hearing her confess that she had sex once.

"Marshon gave me an ecstasy pill one night, and it made me really horny. When he came at me, I didn't turn him down, and we didn't use protection. I am so sorry Fahan. I swear I'm sorry, and I would never intentionally hurt you. I chose you over my own baby. I didn't want a child with Nico. All I want is you."

I had to get away from her. All that crying she was doing was agitating the fuck out of me. She could have sat me down and told me this shit way sooner, but she waited until she was going to get caught. She only confessed because she had to, much like the situation with Vickie and Azaan. The crazy thing about it was, I was away for more than a year. Had Dior came to me on some grown woman shit and admitted to having sex one time, I probably would have been mad, but I'm sure I would have forgiven her. She's only human, and I left her out here alone. My time was like a punishment to her too in the sense that she couldn't have sex or be affectionate with anyone. Yeah, we can live without sex, but we're human. Just like men get horny, I know women do too.

She could have sat me down and put everything on the table, but she was going to be sneaky and try to get away with it. Nico's messy ass put her business out there for the world to see, and now she cared about me knowing. She still didn't totally confess. She started out on some bullshit trying to get me to believe that the messages were fake. My girl didn't just have sex with a nigga. She let him hit her raw, and she got pregnant by the dude. I turned to walk towards the closet. I needed to get out of that apartment before I did some shit I might regret. I didn't want to talk, and I didn't want to hear any more of what Dior had to say.

"Fahan, please talk to me," she begged as I put my sneakers on.

I ignored her and pulled a shirt over my head. I turned around and headed for the dresser to get my keys. She called herself blocking me, but I nicely stepped around her.

"Fahan, please!"

She could scream at the top of her lungs. I didn't give a fuck. Not one. I left the apartment and got in my car. I was going to the club, but I texted Azaan to see if he was at home, and he was. I headed in the direction of his townhouse. Times like this, I wished I'd gotten my own shit instead of coming home and living with Dior. As I pulled up in his driveway, I got an email. After checking it, I saw that the publisher that I signed with had sent me a cover and a release date for the book that I had written while I was locked up. I could admit that since being free, I hadn't done a lot of writing, but I still had some time to get it done. I looked at the cover and felt a sense of pride, but I couldn't even get too happy. I was just that pissed. Dior had violated and worse than violating, she'd played me like a sucka. That shit hurt when it came from them broads that you thought were good girls.

Azaan must have seen me pull up because he opened the door before I even rang the bell. "What's good?" he asked. He didn't have a shirt on, and there were some motivational and business books on the couch.

"Did I interrupt bruh?"

"Nah. It's time for me to take a break anyway. I been reading for an hour. What's going on?"

I sat down on the couch and let out an angry chuckle. "You know this bitch Dior fucked a nigga and got pregnant by him right before I came home? The broad had an abortion. Her lil' gay ass friend that used to live with her done posted shit all over Instagram, and blog sites been having a field day with it. Shorty got me out here looking dumb. These muhfuckas even found my page and been tagging me in shit."

Azaan's eyes widened in surprise, and he brought his fist up over his mouth. "Yooooo are you serious right now? Nigga." He reached over and picked up a small glass jar filled with weed that had been sitting on his coffee table. "We gotta smoke to this my G."

As Azaan rolled the blunt, I broke everything down to him. How it had all played out with Dior and what she told me. When I was done, he pulled a lighter from his pocket and set fire to the end of the blunt. "I sat in that cell many days wondering if she'd given the pussy up to anybody. I knew the shit was a very real possibility. All I asked was that she didn't do it on no sucka shit. Don't have a nigga laying in the bed that I was coming home to, don't let the visits and letters slack, don't stop answering the phone for a nigga, and she didn't do any of that. I tried to tell myself that she kept it hood with a nigga, so if she fucked off once or twice, I wouldn't trip too bad but bruh, another nigga got my girl pregnant?" I wanted to punch something or somebody. Dior shitted on me like a muhfucka, and it didn't feel good.

Azaan hit the blunt twice back to back and passed it to me. "I'm sorry to hear that bro. I popped up on her a few times, and she never had company or no shit. You know women are sneaky as fuck, look at Vickie. I don't know what she was doing or how often she was doing it, but her getting pregnant by the nigga puts things in an entirely different perspective. Like, got damn, you couldn't make the nigga use a condom?"

I hit the blunt furiously. "Exactly," I replied, my voice strained from holding weed smoke in my lungs. "She just let a nigga skeet all in her, and I'm not supposed to feel disrespected?" I shook my head angrily, exhaled the smoke, and hit the blunt again.

"Damn. Looks like we're both having woman troubles."

"You still haven't talked to Jayda?"

"Nah. I'm just letting her chill. I know how she can get. She was already hesitant to rock with me like that because she was still grieving. I don't know man, maybe we weren't meant to be. After shit ended with Vickie, maybe I should have just chilled for a minute."

I puffed from the blunt and passed it back to Azaan. "To think, I was happy to be coming home to my girl. I promised myself that I wasn't gon' be out here wiling. I see dozens of bad chicks every night at the club, and my restraint has been out of this world, but nigga I'm 'bout to go in." For the first time since seeing those IG posts, I calmed down just a tad. I was about to have fun sticking dick to whatever women I chose.

"You breaking up with her or you just putting her on time out?" Azaan inquired.

I kissed my teeth. "If it's aight, I'm gonna stay here with you for a few days. I don't see me going back to her crib, but if I do, it's gon' be after I do me for a lil' bit. I think it's a wrap though bruh. She was pregnant by that man." I stared off into space thinking about my chick getting freaky with the next man off an E pill, while I sat in a prison cell twiddling my thumbs. All for a fuck ass reality show.

"You know you can stay here as long as you need to."

"I appreciate it bro."

* * *

THE BLUNT that I smoked with Azaan had mellowed me out for real, but I was still pissed. Dior was blowing my phone up so much that I blocked her. I didn't have anything good to say to her at the moment. I told Azaan I was going to stay with him, but if things went as planned, I'd be leaving the club getting a hotel room with something bad on my arm. I had been faithful to Dior, and being faithful wasn't the easiest thing in the world. Not when you're handsome and fly as hell and women throw themselves at you often. I had resisted all temptation though, but that shit was a wrap. Still, I was going to take heed to what Azaan said and not deal with any of the strippers. The club was doing good, and the last thing I needed was drama. I might get at one of the patrons though. Women came to the club just like men did, and not all of them were gay or bi-sexual. The club just had a cool, laid back atmosphere that people liked. In a few weeks, Azaan and I had rapper Da Baby coming, and we knew the shit was going to be epic. Tickets were already selling out.

I had gotten to the club an hour before any of the other staff had to arrive. I went over some paperwork, ordered some liquor and food, and then I hit the bar and fixed myself a stiff drink. As I sipped my liquor, I scrolled through my IG page amazed at all the females that were on my ass since I'd been tagged in all of Dior's bullshit. Maybe they knew I would see the shit and dump her or maybe they didn't care if I was taken, because my DMs were blowing up, and some of those chicks were bad. One female with 21.5k followers was on me hard. it was baffling to me. I even had some comments from local women saying they were going to come check the club out, and I told them to pull up. I couldn't be too mad if the situation was bringing me potential pussy and business. It dawned on me that I should post my book cover. Since my followers were going up, I was gon' use it to my advantage.

I didn't care about likes or any of that other trivial social media shit, but if the followers I was getting was going to equate to dollars in my pocket, then I was with it. I posted my book cover and drained all the liquor from my glass. By the time I fixed myself another drink and sat back at the bar, I had 39 likes. I shook my head. Social media was wild. If used the right way, it could definitely be a good tool. I could see why some chicks took it so seriously.

The door opened, and I looked up and saw Liah walking in. When our eyes met, I could see the embarrassment in her face. She knew that I knew about what went down with her and Azaan. I wasn't staring at her because I felt no kind of way about her, I was staring at her because she was pretty as hell, and it was hard for me to believe she used to be out there like that. Her hair was slicked back in a long weave ponytail. Her long lashes brought out her chinky eyes, and her naturally pink lips made it look like she had gloss on. My eyes roamed over her body, and she was almost bursting out of her black work pants. Her hips and thighs were juicy, and shorty wasn't missing no meals.

"What's up?" I asked when she looked away. I loved my brother, and I was gon' always ride with him. He wasn't wrong for shooting Liah. He wasn't even wrong for not caring for her or for not trusting her but since I didn't know the drugged out Liah and I had only met the quiet and meek one, I couldn't bring myself to dislike her.

"Hi," she stated sheepishly. Liah looked so uncomfortable that I had to smile.

"Relax ma. I'm not the big bad wolf. We're good."

She breathed a sigh of relief. "Um, I want to put in my two-week notice. Since you now know about my past, I don't have to front like the money I was making as a cocktail waitress wasn't good. I appreciate Azaan for giving me a job even though he doesn't care for me, but I think I want to work at a club where no one knows me and I can be a waitress."

I took a sip from my drink and studied her thick frame. "You can be a cocktail waitress here. I'll talk to my brother. I don't know you that well, but I'm doing you this favor because I believe in giving people second chances. All of us have a less than perfect past. Don't make me regret it Liah. On God, I'm not threatening you, but I can be as ruthless as my brother. Before you ever cross us, just quit. You got that?"

She nodded. "I got it. Thank you so much."

"I'll tell Eva that tonight is your last night in the kitchen."

She smiled and told me thank you once again. Liah headed towards the kitchen as more staff started filing in. I couldn't help but to watch her ass as she walked off. Maybe I was tripping but ex-fiend or not, I'd hit that.

# DIOR

I drove towards my friend Dana's house so mad that I'm surprised I wasn't breathing fire. I'd cried for so many hours that my eyes were swollen, and my voice was hoarse. Producers from the show, Marshon, friends, everyone had been blowing up my phone except the person that I wanted to hear from. Fahan was furious with my ass, and I couldn't even blame him. I'd messed up bad. I wasn't even sure he would forgive me and for that, Nico had to get it. I saw on social media that he was at Dana's and at that point, I didn't care about him being a man. Nico had to see me. He was talking big shit on social media until I stooped down to his level of petty and uploaded screenshots of text messages between us where he talked about having herpes. The bumpy dick punk got mute after that shit, but I still wasn't satisfied. Even though Nico was bigger than me and a man, I knew if I could get the upper hand, I could do enough damage for him to know that I'd been there.

When I pulled up in front of Dana's house, she and Nico were on her porch. Nico probably assumed I was coming to confront him. Since he was a man, he wouldn't be expecting me to try and fight him, so he'd be somewhat unguarded. If I had a gun I'd shoot him in the ass, and that's no lie. I cuffed my mace in my hand and hopped out of the car. Dana and

Nico eyed me. As soon as I made it up to the porch, Nico began flapping his dick sucking lips.

"All this drama could have been avoided. I was drunk as hell, and I didn't mean to do all that while we were taping, but you didn't even let me apologize. You just straight kicked me out knowing I didn't have anywhere to go. You knew that was gon' piss me off, so yeah, I did some foul shit, but you—"

He was so busy talking, he didn't notice what I was doing. I brought my hand up and sprayed mace directly in his eyes. Nico screamed and hopped up out of the chair so fast that it toppled over, and that was my opportunity. While he couldn't see, I pushed his big ass hard as I could and he tripped over the chair and fell backwards. I ran up on him and started beating the shit out of him. I threw a good six or seven punches landing on his face and on his head before Dana pulled me off of him. I knew there was a chance Nico would retaliate and do some foul shit like slash my tires or get some girls to jump me, but I didn't care. He cost me my relationship with Fahan, and I was out for blood.

"You dumb ass, wack ass bitch," Nico screamed as he struggled to get up off the ground. His eyes were bloodshot red, and tears were streaming down his face. "Dana bring me some water! Oh my gahhh bitch, you really playing dirty. It's on now. That's yo' ass Dior."

"Nigga fuck yo' fat ass. You better be glad it's me here. You know Fahan is private as hell and you got all these gossip pages tagging him. I had to talk him out of beating yo' ass and honestly, if he sees you it still might be on. I suggest you don't come to our crib on the dumb shit because he just wants a reason," I bluffed. It was a lie, but after the fact, I thought about how Nico could roll up causing trouble and get me evicted. I wanted him to be scared to come around me with the bullshit.

"Oh, don't worry baby. I'm not gon' come to the house and trespass, that will give your felon a reason to bust his lil' gun, but best believe, I'm gon' catch you in the streets. I might be a sissy, but I'm still a man, and I'm gon' beat the brakes off you."

"Fuck you bitch," I spat and walked off the porch towards my car. Attacking Nico really hadn't made me feel any better.

Tears streamed down my face as I pulled off. I wasn't even sure where I was going. After about thirty minutes of driving aimlessly around, I ended up at a bar. Flipping my visor down, I swiped my hands across my cheeks to erase the tears that were flowing. I studied my reflection. I looked horrible, but oh well. I was going inside to get some drinks. I needed to drink the pain away. It didn't matter to me if I got so drunk that I had to take an Uber home. I just wanted to forget the look of disgust that Fahan had tossed my away after I told him about Marshon, the pregnancy, and the abortion. Fahan had never looked at me with such contempt, and it made my heart hurt. If he forgave me, I would never so much as even smile at another man. All I wanted was him. Marshon was fine and with each passing day his music was becoming more popular, and his fan base was growing, but he still wasn't Fahan. I could have gotten away with pretending everything was scripted if Nico hadn't uploaded proof for the world to see. I hated him more than I'd ever hated anyone in my life.

In an effort to improve my appearance, I put lip gloss on my lips and covered my puffy eyes with shades. That would just have to do. I wasn't going inside to meet anybody. I was going in there to drown my sorrows. If Fahan didn't take me back, I'd be single for a very long time. The thought of being with another man saddened me. Inside the bar, I ordered a mixed drink and some wings. I didn't really have an appetite but on top of the way I was already feeling, I didn't want to get sick from drinking on an empty stomach. Once the bartender placed the drink in front of me, I took a large sip. Tired of my phone going off from social media notifications, I logged out of everything. I didn't want to turn my phone off because I was still praying that Fahan would call after he calmed down. He hadn't taken any of his belongings with him, so he had to come back to the apartment sooner or later.

My heart rate increased as I thought about the fact that Fahan might come home while I wasn't there. I damn near tossed some money on the bar and ran out of there, but I needed the alcohol. The few sips that I had were already somewhat calming me down. I had devoured the entire drink and ordered a second drink when my wings came out. I didn't touch them until my second drink was gone. I was good and tipsy. One more would get me where I needed to be. I ordered drink number three and started fucking those wings up while I waited. The alcohol had me convincing myself that Fahan loved me and that even though he was angry, he wouldn't just up and leave me like that. Dana called my phone and I started not to answer it, but I decided that I would. She was a neutral friend, and she might tell me if Nico was planning something. Since he had it out for me, I couldn't get caught slipping.

"Hello?" I didn't want her to know how miserable I was or that Fahan had left me.

"Are you okay? Girl, you and that Nico are a hot mess. He just left here. It took me forever to calm him down. He was hotter than fish grease honey, but like I told him even before you came over here, he was dead wrong. He was your friend, and you got him on that show. For him to say some shady shit like that in front of the cameras was some messed up shit. You don't throw your friends under the bus like that for fifteen minutes of fame and some bitches that you don't know. He tried to act hard at first, but he had just started to see things my way and was talking about apologizing when you pulled up."

"Fuck his apology," I snarled with tears in my eyes. Hearing her say that he had in fact done me wrong made me emotional. I thought he was my friend, and Nico really played me. Yeah I did Fahan wrong but damn, my friend was supposed to have my back. Just like Dana said, his messy ass did that for fifteen minutes of fame. I hope it was worth it.

"I think he's lowkey worried that Fahan is going to come after him. You know Nico isn't a punk when it comes to fighting, but he not about that gun play. That nigga is scared on the low."

"Good. He better be, because Fahan is super pissed."

"Are you okay though?"

"Yeah. I'm meeting Fahan at a bar, and he just walked in. I'll call you later."

"Okay boo." I ended the call and downed my third drink. I drank that shit down so fast that by the time the glass was empty, I was damn near seeing double. Extra bothered that Fahan hadn't called me, I decided to pop up at the club. He had cooled down enough that he was gon' talk to my ass if I had to force it out of him.

The club still had two hours before it closed, so I had time to run home and take a shower. I'd been through the most, and I would feel better if I pulled up on him looking like something. I was drunk, but I still had the good sense to follow the speed limit. In fact, I think I was driving a little below the speed limit. I wasn't trying to get in an accident, and I for damn sure didn't want to get a DUI. Once I arrived at home, before getting in the shower, I rolled a blunt and smoked half of it. Yes, I was trying to get shit faced. I wasn't even going to drive to the club. I would take an Uber, and if things went well, Fahan would be the one taking me home. He had hours to calm down. Even though I messed up, he was my man, and we loved each other. He couldn't just cut me off with no kind of communication ever again. Nah, I wasn't going to let him do me like that.

After I got out of the shower, I dressed in tight black jeans, a fitted, white V-neck tee, and some wheat-colored Timberlands. I stared at my reflection and smiled. That's why I wanted to get so drunk and so high. It was the only thing that had managed to stop the tears. In my altered mind state everything was going to be okay between Fahan and I. We might have to argue a little more, I may have to grovel a little more, and then hopefully we could have some good ass make-up sex. If things really went the way I wanted them to, I'd be pregnant by Fahan within the next month or two. I knew that it had to hurt him that I got pregnant by some random ass nigga, and I was sorry for that shit.

After I ordered the Uber, I got the notification that he was ten minutes away. I got comfortable on the couch and since I was in a better head space, I logged back into my social media. What I saw literally made me stop breathing for a few seconds. I held my breath as I scrolled through all the tags and comments about how women were loving Fahan. It also showed him in the comments flirting with women, and it was being insin- uated that he was available. I wanted to throw my phone, but I remained calm. I had to remind myself that Fahan was fresh out of prison and mad at me. Of course, he was going to have a little bit of fun, but I hoped those bitches knew, it was going to be short-lived. I was getting my man back.

I kissed my teeth and frowned my face up at the thirsty ass women in the comments. They were really pathetic, and it turned my stomach to see Fahan flirting back with a few of them. Everyone that he replied to, I went to their page and if the account wasn't private, I lurked on their page. Numbness from the weed and liquor was the only thing that kept me from crying when I saw how gorgeous some of those women were. One of them was the ex of a famous rapper. These were the kinds of hos that were throwing the pussy at Fahan. I'd never been insecure and I knew I was a pretty woman, but I'd be lying if I said some of them weren't way badder than me. To say that I was intimidated would be an understatement.

The Uber finally came, and I continued lurking on social media after getting in the car. My eyebrows dipped low from confusion when I went to one of Fahan's most recent posts and saw that he'd uploaded a book cover, and he had a book coming out in the next few weeks. He didn't even tell me. With trembling hands, I screenshot the post and posted the book cover on my page. My fingers moved fast as hell as I typed a caption.

*Don't ever get it twisted, this gon' be my nigga always and forever!!! I don't care what we go through or what it looks like, that's me!! I did some dumb shit while he was away, and I have to make up for it, but no man can nor will they ever compare to this man right here. He has a book coming out soon. Y'all thirsty bitches go cop that!!!*

I put my phone in my lap and tried to compose myself. I had to remember that I was the one in the wrong, and I couldn't go up to him on no rah rah type shit. The closer we got to the club, the more anxious I became. I took slow, deep breaths to calm my nerves. We arrived, and I thanked the driver and got out of the car. When I reached the door, I didn't even waste time trying to explain that I was the owner's girl. I just paid to get in. Once I was inside the packed club, I looked around for Fahan. I saw mad niggas everywhere of course, but what really caught my eye was the ladies. The fully clothed ones and the strippers. Every female that I saw, was pretty. I knew that my man owned a strip club, duh, but I never really gave too much thought to what the dancers looked like. A pretty light-skinned female sauntered by and her ass was so huge, I had to do a double take. I was starting to feel sick. While I was fucking up, there were some bad ass chicks out there waiting to take my place. My man was a hot commodity.

I made my way through the crowd, and I didn't see Fahan at first, so I kept looking. I wasn't sure where the office was, and I knew if I tried to locate it on my own, I would be stopped by security. Security! That gave me a thought. I located the nearest bouncer and walked up to him. "Hi, my name is Dior. Fahan is my boyfriend. Can you ask him to come out here please?"

He eyed me. "Sure thing."

The bouncer moved away from me some as he pulled a walkie talkie off his hip and began to speak into it. I prayed that Fahan wouldn't tell him to toss my ass out into the street. I became entranced watching a thick ass dark-skinned stripper take over the stage. The men were loving her. Her braids were pulled up into a high ponytail, and the braids still brushed back and forth across her ass as she walked. She was bad as hell. Damn, when Fahan and I got back together, I was going to have to try and get him to spend less time at the club. These women were making me insecure as hell. Compared to them, I was built like a teenaged white girl. The bouncer came over and snapped me from my thoughts.

"He's on his way out."

I gave him a bright smile. "Thank you." I really wanted to ask why he hadn't just told me to send me into the office, but he wouldn't know why Fahan said what he said, so that would be pointless. I just couldn't get over the fact that all my skeletons came tumbling out of the closet and now my man hated me. Even in the crowded club, I smelled his cologne before I saw his face. I turned my head to the left and there he was. My fine ass Fahan. With the way his jaw muscles were clenched together, I could only gather that he was still mad.

He approached me, grabbed my arm gently, and guided me towards the door. "What are you doing? Fahan, we need to talk."

"I'm at work. Whatever you have to say to me, you have five minutes to say it." He pushed the door open, and we walked through it.

"Five minutes, Fahan why can't I just come in your office? I know I messed up, but why are you treating me like this?" I refused to cry, but I wasn't above begging.

"You better be glad I'm treating you like *this*, because if I was less of a man I'd put my foot in yo' ass," he seethed. Rage flickered in his eyes, and I knew that he was for sure being honest with me. At the moment, Fahan looked like he'd love nothing more than to slap the taste out of my mouth.

"It was one time Fahan. I didn't have sex but one time, and I held you down for one year and damn near six months. That doesn't count for anything?"

"And that one time that you had sex you went all out huh? Niggas nutting in you and getting you pregnant and shit. You turned up for real." He smirked.

"How many times can I say I'm sorry?"

"You can stop saying you're sorry because that shit don't mean anything to me, but dig this. For the moment, I'm single. You had that one time to do you, so let me do me. I'm 'bout to be out here fucking off and enjoying a little freedom. Once I'm done, if my feelings have changed, we can talk about working on us."

It was my turn to want to smack fire out of his ass. Fahan was being real bold, but what could I say? I'd done my dirt, been sloppy with it, and gotten caught. All I could do was listen as he told me that he was about to be out here wildin' and fucking other women. I put my head down and ordered an Uber. There was nothing else I could say. Fahan was a stubborn man, and if he was dead set on getting me back, that's what he was gon' do.

"We done here?" he asked.

"Yeah, we're done," I stated, fighting back tears. I lost my man, and for what?

# AZAAN

"**W**hat's good with you?" I asked Vickie after she opened the door for me. I was getting really tired of her theatrics. Something had to give. Her mom had called me all hysterical and shit so I hopped on a flight. Not necessarily for Vickie but for my son.

"What do you mean?" she asked with a tear streaked face.

I brushed past her and entered her house. "Fuck you mean what I mean? Don't play with me. Your moms called me all upset talking about how you asked her to pick Aheem up from daycare and how you were insinuating that you were gon' kill yourself. Do I need to take my lil' man back to North Carolina while you get your mind right?" The sight before me was borderline pathetic.

Instead of Vickie taking accountability for her actions, admitting she fucked up, putting on her big girl panties and getting on with life, she kept pulling all this extra bullshit for sympathy and attention. I had none for her. Not one ounce.

"While I get my mind right?" She jerked her head back and screwed up her face. "All you care about is Aheem huh? I could shoot myself in the head and you wouldn't even care, would you?"

I passively shrugged one shoulder. "It would be fucked up but I mean, if you want to take your own life that's what it is. Just don't do it while my son is here."

Vickie looked at me like I had two heads. "I always knew you were heartless, but got damn Azaan. I gave birth to your son and you don't give a fuck about me. How does that work?"

"Nah, I actually gave a fuck about you. I loved your ass. I provided well for you, and I tried to be the best nigga that I knew how. I fucked up sometimes because I'm human. For the most part, I watched how I moved in the streets because I loved you enough to not want none of these muhfuckas in the city to be able to laugh and say I had you out here looking stupid. I worked on becoming a better me for you and my son, and for years you lied to me about knowing my cousin, you snuck behind my back and sent him money, visited him in prison, you killed the nigga, and then you fucked another nigga in my bed. You been dead to me, so killing yourself won't change much. This is the last time I'm gon' tell you to get your shit together. If you don't, my son will be in North Carolina with me."

"And the police will be at every trap spot you own. The ones in Miami and in North Carolina. If I can't have you, nobody will. I'll let you rot in prison before I watch you with the next bitch," Vickie screamed with her eyes full of tears.

I rushed up in her personal space so fast and aggressively that I bumped her with my chest. "Oh, you got a death wish for real. First you fuck a nigga in the bed I bought and now you threatening me with the police?" I wrapped my hands around her neck and squeezed with all my might. "I will kill the fuck out of you bitch," I stated through clenched teeth. "You got that shit?" Spit flew from my mouth as I talked.

Vickie's eyes rolled in the back of her head, and I released her just as her body grew limp. She fell to the floor crying and gasping for air. I knelt down to be at eye level with her. I grabbed her face with my hand and made her look at me. "The next time I won't stop until you're blue in the face. My son is going back to North Carolina with me. You can get him back when you stop being a pathetic nut job. The next time you threaten me with the police, I'll cut your mom's head off and make you watch me, ho."

I let her face go, stood up and left. All I needed was to get my son from daycare. I could chill at my aunt Joie's house until I booked us a flight back to North Carolina. She still wasn't in good shape since Meer's disappearance, and I knew she might enjoy the company. I was trying really hard not to kill my son's mother, but Vickie was on thin ass ice. If she knew how close she was to dying at my hands, she'd be shocked as fuck.

* * *

TWENTY-FOUR HOURS LATER, I was at home with Aheem. I had decided to keep him for a while, so I was online reading the reviews of different daycares. I would let Fahan run the club so I could be home with him at night, but I wanted him in school for at least a few hours a day. Not for them to teach him, because I did that very well. I felt it was important for him to be around other kids his age. I didn't want my kid growing up to be weird and anti-social. His third birthday was coming up, and I also needed to plan something special for him. I didn't know anyone like that in North Carolina so there wouldn't be a party.

I fed him dinner, gave him a bath, read him a story, and chilled with him till he fell asleep. I then stepped outside on my front porch and sparked a much needed blunt. I shout out all single mothers because having to be the sole provider and make sure kids are straight isn't an easy task. I was blessed in the sense that I could make money several different ways from the comfort of my own couch. Shit was sweet like that, but I knew a lot of people weren't in that same position. Vickie's dumb ass had it made. I provided her every need, provided for my son, and spoiled the hell out of both of them. All she had to do every day was wake up and do whatever it was that she wanted to do. Shorty got her hair done once a week. She got facials once a month, went to the nail shop every two weeks. She was forever getting her teeth whitened or buying clothes. Vickie acted like she was a real life Ms. America or some shit, and I never complained. I just footed the bill. She wasn't getting my son back until she got her mind right, and that was facts. I didn't care how long I had to keep him with me. I also didn't care how many times her mother or her sister called my phone. Aheem was my son.

Halfway through my blunt I saw bright headlights. When I looked up, I peeped a G wagon pulling into a parking space. Jayda. With all that was going on, I hadn't had too much time to dwell on what happened with us, but I'd be lying if I said I wasn't missing shorty. I had done enough chasing her though. If she truly wanted to keep dealing with me, she'd have to come to me. I watched as she got out of her whip and walked over to me. She was dressed in blue leggings and a matching blue, cropped Champion sweatshirt. On her feet were some dope ass blue and black sneakers. Her long weave was in loose curls and draped over her breasts. Shit had to be about twenty inches. Pink gloss painted her lips and I could see those freckles underneath the moonlight. She stopped in front of me.

"Did I catch you at a bad time?"

"Nah. My son is in there asleep, so I came out here to smoke. Drama with his moms as usual," I mumbled. "How you been though? You look good." I hit the blunt as I looked up at her.

"I've been doing a lot of thinking. So much so that I'm tired of thinking. I just want my head to be one big empty space."

I let out a chuckle. "Shit, I'm with you on that."

"Is it unrealistic of me though? Like, just for right now, I just want to be. I don't want to talk about you, Liah, or anything else. I'm tired Azaan."

I put my blunt out. "That's fine with me. You good though?" I looked over at her, and she nodded. "I missed you. I was trying to give you your space, but a nigga dead ass been missing you."

"I miss you too. Even when I don't want to."

I stood up and reached for her hand. I pulled her up, and we walked inside my townhouse. I needed something to drink after smoking, so I headed for the kitchen. "You want something to drink?" I called out.

"Yeah. A bottle of water please."

I got our drinks and headed back into the living room. We were quiet for a moment, half-watching some show. At some point, I realized my dick was hard from being so close to Jayda. I leaned in and kissed her on the neck. She turned her head towards mine and our lips met. I parted hers with my tongue and pulled her into my lap. Jayda broke the kiss. She stared down at me. She appeared nervous as she chewed on her bottom lip. I palmed her ass. "What's wrong?" She said she didn't want to talk about heavy shit, but it looked like she had some heavy shit on the tip of her tongue.

"I'm pregnant."

"Word?" I'm grown, so I knew how babies were made. I wasn't surprised, but I knew how Jayda was. If she told me that she didn't want to have my kid because she was still grieving Biggs, that shit would surely piss me off. I wanted to handle the situation delicately. "How you feel about that?" I asked, preparing myself to not like her answer.

"I'm feeling like in the next eight months, I'm gonna be somebody's mother. How do you feel about that?"

I smiled. "I feel like for the next eight months, I get to feed you, and watch your belly grow, and prepare for my second child, get on your nerves, and fuck that juicy pregnant pussy every chance I get."

Jayda laughed. "You are a special case."

"That I am." I licked my lips. "So you forgive me? For everything?"

Jayda nodded. I scooted to the edge of the couch and stood up. With her legs wrapped around my waist, I headed for my bedroom where I proceeded to make love to my baby mama.

28

# LIAH

One of the best things I'd ever done was come out of the kitchen
to become a cocktail waitress. Even on a slow night, I could
leave the club with more than $200. My dad was so happy that
I was still sober that he did nice things for me all the time. One day, he
sent me edible arrangements. Another day, he stopped by randomly and
gave me a gift certificate to a nail salon. I was loving my newfound relationship with my parents. We were definitely making up for lost times. I
did dinner with them every Sunday, and Jayda and I hung out at least once
a week. I had even gone on a second date with Derrin. Life was pretty
straight. I hadn't seen Leslie since I paid him his money, and I had no
complaints about life.

I walked over to the bar and the bartender, Sheila, handed me a cup of
dark liquor. "Take this to the office please. Fahan asked for it about fifteen
minutes ago. We've been swamped."

"Okay."

I knew from Jayda that Azaan had his son. For that reason, he hadn't been
to the club in a few days, so it was just Fahan. He was cool as fuck, and I
genuinely liked him. I'd never had a job before the club, so I didn't have a
lot of experiences with bosses, but I knew he was a good one. I actually

164

enjoyed work and if they were short staffed, I didn't mind coming in on my nights off.

The office door wasn't closed all the way, and I walked in on Fahan getting head. "Ummmmmmm," he groaned as I assumed he came, and the chick on her knees kept right on bobbing her head.

"Fuck, sorry," I mumbled and jumped back out the door. Once I could no longer see him, I placed one hand over my racing heart. Superhead in there didn't seem to care, but I hoped that Fahan wasn't mad that I walked in on him. I guess I should have knocked.

I waited for my heart rate to go back to normal while I pondered waiting or just leaving. After a few minutes, the chick came out of the office with a smirk on her face. She was a pretty girl with almond-colored skin and a short haircut. I had learned from a gossip blog on Instagram that Fahan's ex was on a reality show. I read all the tea that went down with them, and it was interesting to say the least. I found myself staring at his pictures for the longest time. I knew a man like him would never want me, but that didn't mean I couldn't admire him.

Even though he was in the office alone, I knocked before entering. "Come in."

When I walked in, Fahan was sitting behind his desk. "Sorry about that."

He smiled. "Ain't shit." He reached for the drink in my hand. I could only gather that he wasn't too hurt from what his ex did because at least two nights out of the week, I saw Fahan leaving the club with a different woman.

"Can I ask you a quick question?" I cocked my head slightly to the left and observed him as he sipped his drink.

"What's good?"

"You seem like a guy that keeps it a hundred, and I don't have a lot of experience with guys like that. Aside from trying to milk them for money. If I've only gone out on two dates with a guy, and I want to surprise him with a nice dinner at a nice restaurant for his birthday, is that doing too much?"

"Yes," he answered the question with no thought or hesitation.

I raised my eyebrows. "Okayyyy."

Fahan chuckled. "I mean, it's only jumping the gun because you don't know if he already has plans. If he hasn't asked you to do anything with him for his birthday, then he probably already does have plans. That doesn't mean they're plans with another female, but I know how y'all women get. When you're feeling a guy, you want to do holidays and special days and all that shit, and then if he doesn't spend that day with you, you feel some type of way. If he already has plans and you surprise him with some shit and he tells you he can't do it, you're gonna be disappointed. If you want to do something nice for him, just get him a simple gift and let him get it at his own leisure."

I nodded. "That's pretty good advice. Thanks."

"No problem."

I left the office planning on doing just what he said. I wasn't going to assume that Derrin wanted to spend his birthday with me.

* * *

"CAN YOU DO ME A FAVOR?" a pretty female asked me after I served the bottles that she and her group ordered to VIP.

"Yeah sure, what's up?" I was used to men getting booths, and most times, they would have women in the booths with them. However, sometimes women copped the booths. I wasn't sure who this female was, but her and five of her homegirls were in VIP partying and ordering bottles like it wasn't anything. They were all dressed to impressed and a few of them had on some serious ice. They must have been dope dealers' girls or some shit.

Shorty licked her lips seductively. "That fine ass boss of yours, the one with the tattoo on his face, let him know that one of his VIP guests wants to holler at him about something very important." I could tell from the lustful glare she was giving me, that she wanted to fuck Fahan. I didn't blame her.

She was about 5'8 with peanut butter-colored skin. She had long wet-n-wavy weave in her head and on her body was a tight, black bodycon dress. She had an iced-out Cartier watch on her wrist, and her stiletto-shaped nails were so long, I wondered how she wiped her ass good. She had on a ton of make-up. She was one of those girls that was pretty with all that make-up on, but I could tell she was average looking with it off.

I winked at her. "Sure thang."

"Thank you boo." She reached out and squeezed my arm.

When I got to the bar to collect the rest of my orders, Fahan was behind the bar talking to one of the bartenders. I waited for him to finish. "You have an admirer in the booth by the stage. Ole girl in the black bodycon dress."

He looked over in that direction and his eyes roamed the crowd for her. I could tell when he spotted her because he raised his eyebrows. "She aight. Hmm, should I go over there?"

I laughed. "You have to think about it?"

"Mann I never thought I'd say this, but a nigga is tired. I done fucked ten days in a row. I need a break. I might get her number though," he stated as he stroked his chin.

I frowned up my face playfully. "That was TMI."

"Fahan!"

His name was called so aggressively that I instinctively looked over my shoulder to see who it was. I saw the girl that I recognized from the blogs, and she looked pissed. "You really came and got all your shit when I wasn't home?" she yelled.

I turned away and locked eyes with Misty the bartender. She gave me a look, and I went about my business. Fahan had his hands full with that one. I went to make sure all of my customers were happy. We only had an hour left before we closed. A few people had already tipped me, but most people with booths just closed out their tabs at the end of the night. I already had $275 in my possession so any other tips that I got would make me super happy. My parents were worried about me working in the club because they were scared I'd get tempted to drink or do other drugs. Weed was harmless to me but being that I was a recovering addict, weed was too much of a gateway drug for me. I could admit that sometimes I smelled it, and I missed being high off weed, but weed was what started my down-ward spiral, so I always brushed the thoughts off. As far as alcohol, I wasn't even going to pretend that I wanted to go the rest of my life without wine or liquor on occasions, but I hadn't had any yet. I wanted being sober to be a very normal feeling for me. I didn't want anything to turn into something that I needed or desired every day. Except chocolate. Or dick.

I'd been getting horny as hell lately. I hadn't talked to Derrin in a few days, but every night at least one guy in the club always tried me. I was very tempted to give somebody a chance just so I could get my rocks off. I rushed around the club getting everything done so I could get out of there exactly when I was supposed to. Once the club closed, I counted a total of $325 in tips, and I wasn't mad at all. I grabbed my belongings and walked out with a few of the bartenders. Fahan and old girl were out in the parking lot. He looked frustrated as shit.

"Will you leave me the fuck alone? Please?" he begged in an agitated voice.

I kept my head down and ordered my Uber. "My son is going with his daddy tomorrow, so I can give you a ride home," Misty promised me. She hated for me to take Ubers late night, but she lived thirty minutes away from me and had to get home so her baby-sitter could leave. I didn't hold it against her.

I gave her a small smile. "It's okay boo. I'm okay. I don't live far and if the Uber driver looks creepy, I'll request another one."

"Not tonight," I mumbled as I noticed it was taking a long time for them to connect me with a driver.

"You good?" I heard Fahan's voice. I looked up and he and his ex were looking over at me.

"Um yeah, just ordering an Uber."

"Uber? I got you shorty. I'll give you a ride."

I opened my mouth to tell him it was fine and instantly became irritated with the way his ex was glaring at me. She was looking at me like she hated my guts, and I hadn't done anything to her dumb ass. I started to smile and flirt with him just to get up under her skin, but I didn't have time for the bullshit. "No, that's okay."

"Fuck that. I'm about to leave, and I'm not leaving you standing out here. Get in my car." He pointed his key fob at his car and hit the unlock button.

"You really gon' do that in my face?" Dior screeched.

"Girl, fuck you! I've tried my best to be patient with you, but I can't be nice to you. You won't get it through your thick head that I don't want your ass anymore. Leave me the fuck alone!"

I got inside the car and took a deep breath. I'd never had to deal with any relationship drama. I'd never been in love. Drugs consumed my life at an early age, and they were all that I cared about. If a man didn't want me getting high or refused to contribute to my high, then I'd drop his ass like a bad habit. There wasn't anyone that I cared about more than drugs. So, I'd never experienced what my sister had with Biggs or Azaan.

Fahan got in the car shaking his head. "I'm trying really hard not to put my hands on that girl."

I chuckled. "I live on Cambria Bridge Lane. It's like ten minutes from here."

"Cool. I know where that is."

"I have a confession," I said looking over at Fahan. Damn, he was sexy.

"What's good?"

"I saw your situation on the blogs, and I looked at your page. I got your book when it dropped yesterday, and I stayed up until four in the morning reading it. It's good as hell. You're very talented."

He looked over at me. "Word? That's what's up. Thanks for the support. You stalking a nigga's page and shit." He smiled.

"I'm not stalking you."

"You are if you looking at my shit and didn't follow me. What's your joint, so I can follow you?"

"There's nothing interesting on my page. I just got the hang of social media. When I was in the streets, I didn't care about it. Now, it's a whole new world for me. I can scroll on that shit for hours. It's a bad habit but it passes the time."

"I feel you. I was mad when all that shit popped off with Dior. I never cared about followers and shit, but all them followers I got after I made it to the blogs, that shit got my book sitting at number one. My publisher calling me hounding me about part two. Which is written. I just had to pay somebody to type it up. I'm gon' ride this wave for a lil' minute, but I don't want to be an author like that. Not to drop books on no back to back type shit. I'd be fine with two or three times a year."

"Well you certainly have a gift. I can't wait to read the next part."

"Let me ask you a question. If it's not too personal. How did you get out there on drugs and shit? Like, you didn't grow up in the hood."

"No, I didn't grow up in the hood. I had very well-off parents that had very high expectations for me. I also had very rich and privileged friends that snuck in their mom's pills, coke, and whatever else they could find in the house. I took my first Xan when I was fifteen. It made me feel so good. Like, I didn't care that my dad was yelling at me about failing a test, I didn't feel guilty that I didn't want to go to cheer practice. I just didn't care. I was tired of studying hard. Looking back, I was just dumb as shit. A lazy ass kid that had the world at her feet and thought rebelling was cool. The Xans were too hard to keep getting, so I started smoking weed. It did the trick. All I cared about was getting high. I felt cool. My grades started slipping so my parents kept me grounded which led to me sneaking out of the house. I was just a bad ass. Every time I snuck out or got kicked out, I ended up with a friend that had weed and then one day pills and finally coke. I sniffed coke for the first time, and it was over from there."

"Aye, one thing you see a lot of in the county jail is niggas in there detoxing. Shitting, vomiting, seizing, all kinds of shit because they're going cold turkey from alcohol, lean, pills, coke, or whatever their vice is. There are a whole lot of people out here addicted to shit. You for sure weren't alone. Shit, when I got locked up, that first week without weed, I was ready to break somebody's jaw just for looking at me the wrong way. Too many people use drugs and alcohol to cope. You were already young and impressionable, and that shit just got a hold of you. You shouldn't feel bad though. You should be proud of yourself that you overcame that shit."

"Thank you. You know the crazy thing is, your brother is kind of the reason that I'm clean. I detoxed while I was in a coma. When I woke up, of course it was still hard but there wasn't a lot that I could do while I was stuck in the hospital. In a crazy way, everything worked out in my favor. I just have to keep it up." I wasn't sure if Fahan caught the hint of nervousness in my voice. Relapsing was a real fear of mine. One that I tried to hide from my loved ones.

"You got this." Fahan pulled up at my apartment complex in no time, and I was almost sad that our time together had ended so soon. "Aye, from now on, I'll bring you home at night. It's not far at all, and I don't mind. Don't fix your mouth to say no because I'm not letting you stand outside in the dark every night waiting on an Uber."

"Thanks." I tossed him a smile and got out of the car.

Inside my apartment, I let out a deep sigh. I needed to get some dick fast because there was no way Fahan would even look at me in that way. I honestly believed he was just a nice guy like that, but I don't think my clit was getting the memo. After riding in the car with Fahan, I was hornier than I'd been in a long time. So much so that I got in the shower, closed my eyes, and pleasured myself to visions of his face.

# 29

## JAYDA

"You still don't have an appetite?" Azaan asked as he looked at me with eyes full of sympathy.

I shook my head no. "I'm going to eat some fruit in the car though. If I don't eat anything I'll get lightheaded."

Azaan wrapped his arms around me. "My baby is giving you hell huh? I'm sorry."

I had just finished throwing up, and from there I brushed my teeth and got ready to go to class. I had to take four classes to graduate from law school. Two of them were online and two of them I actually had to go on campus to take. I went by the car rental place every day for a few hours, but I was letting someone else run it for me. Morning sickness was kicking my entire ass. Like I had no freakin' energy whatsoever. It took everything in me just to push through the day. Some days, I felt so weak that I cried.

He kissed me on the lips, and I smirked. "So that means after the baby is born, you have night duties for the first two days after I get home from the hospital?"

"For sure. I'll do it longer than that if you want me to."

I smiled at him. I had really lucked up meeting Azaan. Deeanna was super excited and so were my parents. It wasn't even a question that my baby was going to be spoiled.

"Doctor's appointment tomorrow at noon, right?"

"Yeap." I gave Azaan another kiss and headed out the door to class.

I started my car and popped a strawberry into my mouth. One morning on the way to class, I literally had to pull over and throw up, but I hadn't missed a day of class yet. I was determined to graduate this time around. Nothing was going to stop me. I would graduate when I was five months pregnant, and I was going to wait until my baby was at least three months old before I started applying for jobs. I wanted to spend a lot of time with my baby, and Azaan had enough money that I didn't have to work, but I wanted to work. I didn't let law school kick my ass for nothing.

Aheem was still with Azaan. I wasn't sure what Vickie was in Miami doing, but it wasn't really any of my business. I had agreed to watch after the club for him for a week while he, Aheem, and Fahan went to Haiti to visit family. They were leaving in two weeks, and I really hoped that my morning sickness would be better by then. Even with all of my discomfort, I was grateful for the opportunity to be carrying a child. This was my second chance to have a child by the man that I loved. After already having suffered a miscarriage, I did have a little PTSD. The slightest stomach cramp worried me. I didn't want to speak a bunch of negativity so I kept my fears and concerns to myself, but every day that passed and I was still pregnant, I felt like I reached a milestone. By the time I pulled up at school, all my fruit was gone. I downed a bottle of water, grabbed my bookbag, and exited the car. It was time to go learn and smash some goals, even if I did feel bad.

* * *

"Bae, you killing that banana," Azaan stated as he looked over at me.

I couldn't help but to laugh. "Whatever. Don't watch me. Keep your eyes on the road. All I can eat is fruit or salad. Anything else makes me throw up if I eat it before like five in the evening." I had already eaten blueberries, mangos, and grapes. Now, I was eating a banana. At least my baby liked healthy stuff, but I kind of missed eating shit like pizza and fried chicken. Anything greasy too early in the day was guaranteed to make me throw up, and I was tired of throwing up, so I just ate what agreed with me.

We arrived at the doctor's office, and I got out of the car. It was cold so I was dressed in dark denim jeans, a black hoodie, and sneakers. Over my hoodie I had on a denim jacket. I didn't feel like doing my hair, so my long hair was on top of my head in a messy bun. I didn't have on a lick of make-up. In fact, my eyebrows needed to be waxed terribly. I just didn't have the energy to do the smallest things. When I went to get a Brazilian wax, I had the lady to do my armpits and legs because I'd been too lazy to shave them. I felt like a gorilla with all that body hair, but a part of me didn't even care.

Azaan grabbed my hand and we walked into the office, and I checked in. I wasn't far along at all, and my baby was only the size of a lima bean from what the app on my phone said, but I still wanted to hear the doctor tell me that everything was okay. I never even got to the first ultrasound when I was pregnant by Biggs. This was a first for me, and I was glad that Azaan was there with me. "You talked to Vickie?" I asked as he scrolled through his phone.

Aheem had been with Azaan for a week. Azaan didn't mind at all, but it was weird to me that Vickie wasn't trying to get him back. At first, I thought Azaan didn't hear me because he didn't look up from his phone. As I was about to speak again, he showed me his phone. I didn't understand right away what he was trying to show me, but then it dawned on me that it was Vickie's IG page. I looked through the pictures and saw that the last four pictures had all been of her in the club. On her latest picture, she was even posted up with a rapper. All I could do was shake my head. I wasn't saying that she didn't deserve a break. Azaan should share in the responsibility of raising his child but to my knowledge, she hadn't even called to speak to her son. That was some weirdo shit. I didn't care what I was going through. I'd never abandon my child. Ever.

I handed him the phone back. "Wow."

"Exactly."

The nurse called us to the back, and I got up ready to get the show on the road. After she checked my vital signs, I got on the scale and saw that I'd actually lost three pounds. "Is that going to affect the baby?" Azaan asked.

"No. As long as she's not losing drastic amounts of weight and not dehydrated, the baby will be fine. It is very common for women to lose weight in the first trimester."

We got settled in the room to wait for the doctor, and Azaan and I looked at all of the charts on the wall and informational pamphlets. The doctor came in after about five minutes and got me set up to do the ultrasound. "According to your last period you're about nine weeks, so as you probably know it'll be about another six weeks before we can tell the sex of the baby. Today is just to make sure that everything looks okay."

I nodded and waited nervously for my baby to appear on the screen. She was quiet for about a minute, and that made me very anxious. I was just about to say something when she spoke. "Well Mom and Dad, I have a surprise for you." She pointed at a white mass on the screen. "This is baby A"—she pointed to another mass—"and this is baby B."

My mouth fell open from shock. "You're playing with me. Tell me there are not two babies in my body right now." I was panicking while Azaan shot up out of his chair like a rocket.

"Yooo, say word?"

He was all hype, but he didn't have to carry two babies. That explained why I didn't have any energy. I had two babies in me sucking all of my life force away. He came over to me and kissed me on the lips. "I love you."

I looked at how geeked he was, and I had to smile. After losing one baby, God was now blessing me with two. How could I be mad at that?

# 3 0

## DIOR

I sat home on my couch with my cousin Natalie watching the first episode of the reality show. It was hard for me to enjoy it because the show was ultimately what ruined my life. Well, technically my actions ruined my life, but you get what I'm saying. Nothing too bad happened on the first episode, and Natalie kept gushing over how good I looked. Before the show even went off, I had 1,000 new Instagram followers. I really didn't feel like Fahan was coming back to me, and I tried to tell myself to just focus on getting my bag, but that was hard to do. I missed my man. I missed him something terrible.

My phone rang, and I kissed my teeth seeing that Marshon was calling. I hadn't talked to him since the reunion, and I'd still been ignoring calls from the producers to come back for the second season. The only thing that made me even slightly happy was knowing that a check had come in the mail earlier in the day for $2,500, and I would be getting another one next week. And the week after that and the week after that. Hopefully, my website would get some orders and I would get some hosting gigs because once that money ran out, then what? How could I go from being on TV to working back at some factory or warehouse?

"What?" I snapped into the phone.

"Listen Dior, I know a lot of crazy shit went on, and I'm sorry about that."

"Nigga, fuck you," I spat. "You dead ass set me up. I told you from day one I had a nigga and that I couldn't have him on TV looking crazy. You just didn't give a damn. All for some ratings huh? Now my life is fucked up while your music career is taking off," I yelled into the phone.

"Your life is fucked up my nigga? Oh, so you didn't see all those followers you just got on Instagram and Twitter? My manager hit me and told me to hit you up for him. He wants to represent you. He knows who to reach out to in order to get you hostings. He guaranteed me that he could get you at least $3,500 per gig. With increased followers you can start charging people for promo. On top of that, Kylie is begging me to get you to come back for season two. She said they can give you $6,000 per episode."

I closed my eyes briefly. No amount of money was worth my relationship, but Fahan had made it abundantly clear that he was done with me. No matter how much I cried and begged, he treated me like shit on the bottom of his shoe, so why not get that money? If I could land three club appearances a month, that alone would be $10,500 a month. I for damn sure wouldn't see that much money working a regular job, and I no longer had Fahan to help me out. I hated Marshon's guts, but fuck it.

"Aight, I'm in."

My cousin and I went out for drinks to celebrate. I pushed the drama with Fahan to the back of my mind and decided that maybe it was a blessing in disguise. After four drinks, I was good and lifted. Natalie drove and afterwards she took me home. The liquor did a great job of lifting my spirts because the entire ride back to my apartment, I twerked in the seat. Natalie laughed and rapped along to songs on the radio.

"Bye boo. I'll talk to you later," she stated as I got out of the car.

I was so fucked up that right before I got to my door, I didn't notice a figure in the shadows until it was too late. I saw an arm fly out at me, and I screamed in agony as the flesh on my face was cut open.

# FAHAN

**M**y chest heaved up and down as my semen spilled into the condom. Kat's sexy ass leaned down so that we were chest to chest, and she gently bit my bottom lip. "I could fuck you all day," she moaned before snaking her tongue into my mouth.

Out of all the women I'd had in the short amount of time that I'd been single from Dior, Kat was the most interesting. Her pussy was good as hell, and she had her own bag. She was some kind of beauty influencer, and she made money just from YouTube videos and all of her social media followers. She even promoted my book for me and that shit went from the #4 spot right back to #1. I knew that a lot of social media followers could equate to dollars, but I was blown away when she showed me her latest check from YouTube. Just for one month, she'd made a little over $9,000 from all the views on her videos. Plus, she had partnerships with Fashion Nova, Flat Tummy Tea, and all that other shit. Kat told me that she literally worked two days out of the week and those days consisted of making videos, editing them, uploading them, and taking pictures for her IG page. She made around $15,000 a month and only worked two days a week. I admired the fuck out of that. Shorty was often in the presence of rich niggas, so the fact that she paid for her own flight and made an effort to come see my regular ass was dope.

Kat lived in Brooklyn, but after she got the booth that night at my club and sent Liah to deliver that message, I called her, and we'd been talking on the phone. She surprised me when she flew out to see me. I gripped her waist as we kissed for a moment. Kat had a flight to catch, so I knew round two was out of the question.

She broke the kiss and looked down at me. "When am I going to see you again?"

"I'm not really sure. I'm going to be going to Haiti in the next week. I'll be out there for a week."

Kat bit her bottom lip and looked to be in deep thought. "I'll probably be able to come back out this way in a few weeks. I'm going to Greece for my birthday in two weeks. After that I'll spend a few days catching up on editing and uploading the videos from my trip, and then I'll be free."

I chuckled at her enthusiasm. I for sure didn't see myself being in a relationship in the next few weeks, but I still didn't know if I should be agreeing that far ahead for her to come back out. "We'll definitely be in touch, and we can plan something at the right time."

I assumed that answer satisfied Kat. She eased up off my dick and headed for the bathroom to take a quick shower before heading to the airport. Since I wasn't on good terms with Dior and I had a criminal record, I asked Azaan to get me a crib in his name. I hadn't moved in yet, so I was still staying with him. Kat had paid for a five-star hotel room for her stay in the city, and I was impressed. I'd never fucked with a boss chick before. Shorty spent bread like it was nothing. Without all that make-up she looked totally different. She wasn't ugly, but she looked different. It didn't matter to me though. Like I said, the pussy was good and her having her own bread was a definite plus. Females always hollering they didn't want a broke nigga. Sometimes it's nice for us to meet a woman with money too.

A number that I didn't recognize called my phone, and I sat up to answer it. "Yo." I stood up and pulled the condom from my dick.

"Fahan? This is Natalie. I'm Dior's cousin."

I rolled my eyes upward as soon as I heard Dior's name. That damn girl was the epitome of a stalker. I started to tell ole girl on the phone that I didn't give a damn, but she spoke before I could.

"Dior was attacked last night. We think it was that nigga Nico. He cut her in the face."

"She still in the hospital?"

"No, she's been released. She had to get six stitches—"

I cut her off. "So she's fine? Listen, Dior ain't my problem no more and neither is any of the drama she got herself mixed up in. Don't call my phone about anything concerning her." I ended the call. I'm sure I seemed like an asshole to Natalie, but I really didn't care. Dior did what she did, and I was good on her. The sooner she got that through her head, the better.

* * *

"Okay, I see you," I joked as Liah got in my car. She had her eyebrows done, and she had on some long, dramatic lashes that made her already slanted eyes look even more slanted. She also had red lipstick on. I'd never seen her in anything close to make-up before, and she looked good. I tried to picture what she looked like when she was strung out, but I couldn't.

She smiled bashfully. "The guy I went out on two dates with is a bust, so I guess I should start looking like something so maybe I can find someone else."

I had started giving her rides to and from work. Liah was mad cool. Azaan was still skeptical about her being out of the kitchen, but he'd get over it. I hoped shorty wouldn't make me look stupid after I vouched for her. I needed her to stay on the straight and narrow. Plus, she was looking so good and doing so good. I'd hate for her to mess all that up.

"What happened to him?"

"Well it seems that your advice about not planning anything for his birthday saved me some embarrassment. The man who claimed he was single is pretty much a liar. He uploaded pictures on his birthday of a watch that his girlfriend of three years bought him."

"Damn."

"I mean, I went out on two dates with this man. In public places. Who in the hell does that when they have a girlfriend?"

I shook my head and chuckled. "Niggas do dumb shit sometimes. Pretty much a lot of them want to have their cake and eat it too. That's just life man, but he could have told you something and let you choose. Some women don't mind being side chicks."

Liah raised an eyebrow. "Well I don't want to be a side chick. You said a lot of them want to have their cake and eat it too. You're not like that?"

I shrugged one shoulder. "I didn't cheat on my shorty. The fact that she claims she only had sex once while I was away, I could have forgiven her, but too much happened. She lied too much, and she just played my face. I'm good on that. So now, I'm chilling, and I won't get in another relationship until I know for sure I'm ready to be faithful."

"I can respect that. It's cool though. I'll just take this time to keep focusing on myself. Yayyyyy fun," she stated sarcastically, and I laughed.

"You're definitely a beautiful woman, so it'll happen for sure. I be seeing them niggas on you at the club."

Liah sighed. "I just have to be careful though. Like, I'm not that girl that will tell a man not to smoke or drink or whatever, but I just have to be careful with what I'm around and what I allow into my space. The wrong nigga will have me stressed out and ready to snort some coke."

"Nah, you can't let anybody knock you off your square like that. No matter what these niggas do out here, you gotta stay on ya shit. The best way to shit on a muhfucka that does you wrong is by getting even better after they do you wrong. Show them you didn't need them for shit."

"You make it sound so easy. That's wonderful advice though. Thank you."

"Aye, I'm just here to help."

I pulled up at the club, and it was business as usual. I stayed in my office majority of the night going over paperwork. I wanted everything to be done when I left to go to Haiti. I was excited about seeing my dad and my sisters. Technically, I wasn't supposed to be leaving the country, I wasn't even supposed to leave the state, but my PO was cool as shit. One night she came in, and I let her have all her drinks and her homegirls' drinks on the house. Shorty got shit faced drunk and gave me permission to go. She told me if I got in any trouble I was on my own because she was going to deny giving me permission to go.

When there was only thirty minutes left until close, I decided to go out and make my rounds. Speak to the people and make sure everything was going good. I also liked to personally thank anybody that got VIP booths. Booths brought the club damn good money. People were paying $700 just to sit in booths and have their own lil' section really. As I made my way to the first corner, I saw Liah standing beside some tall light-skinned nigga and he had a bottle of Hennessey hovering over her lips. Her head was tilted back, and he poured the liquor in her mouth in an erotic manner. I raised one eyebrow as I watched the scene unfold. I didn't mind if the girls drank on the job, but they couldn't drink for free. If a nigga wanted to buy any of the girls a drink, he could. As long as they didn't get too fucked up to properly do their job, I was fine with that too. Liah was a different case though.

I watched as ole boy whispered in her ear with one hand on her waist. I wasn't sure what I was feeling. Jealousy? Nah, it couldn't be jealousy because I didn't really look at Liah like that. At least I didn't think I did. She was just a cool female that I respected that was trying to get her shit together. The nigga that had just fed her liquor reached in his pocket and gave her some money, and Liah walked off smiling.

"Hey," she stated when she saw me.

"You think that was a good idea?" I asked.

"What? Me drinking? It was just one shot."

"Yeah okay. I didn't ask you how much it was."

"I appreciate your concern, but I'm fine. It was one swig of liquor; it's not like I snorted a line." She was defensive. "Everybody in here drinks. You don't question them."

"Everybody in here wasn't a fiend."

Liah's head jerked back, and I instantly felt like shit. I didn't mean to call her that, but it was too late to take it back. The look in her eyes was a cross between anger and pain.

"Liah—"

She walked off. I turned around and watched her storm towards the bar. She placed her drink tray down and walked towards the exit. I followed her and by the time I got outside, she was walking towards the street. "Liah!"

I was sure she heard me, but she kept right on walking so I ran after her. "Liah wait! I didn't mean it like that."

She whirled around to face me with tears in her eyes. "You fuckin' meant it! You give me all these fake ass, encouraging ass pep talks and then you say some shit like that to me. You disrespectful ass muhfucka. Fuck you and fuck your brother. I quit."

I ran over to her and blocked her. I grabbed her arms and she hit me in the chest. "Move!"

"No!" I yelled right back at her ass. "I didn't mean it like that. I respect the fuck out of you." I felt like scum watching her cry. I wiped the tears from her face. "Don't do that man. I'm a fucked up ass nigga for saying that shit, and I swear on everything I love, I'm sorry."

"Just let me go. I want to go home."

With damn near no effort, my lips were on hers just that fast. I kissed her hungrily as I eased my tongue into her mouth. I tasted the cognac on her tongue as I kissed her like I just got out of prison. "I'm sorry," I whispered into her mouth. I broke the kiss and cupped her face in my hands. "You forgive me?"

"No."

"What I gotta do?" My eyes searched her face. I didn't want her to relapse 'cus I pissed her off, and I didn't want her feelings to be hurt. Not because I wasn't thinking and said some dumb shit.

"It doesn't matter Fahan."

"It does matter. Tell me what I gotta do?" I stared into her eyes for a minute, and when she didn't answer, I kissed her again. That time was more passionate and more sensual. We stood near the street kissing like we were the only people in the world.

"Go back in the club and wait for me. Okay?"

She nodded, and we walked back to the club. My dick was hard as fuck, but I didn't really have sex on my mind. Kissing her was like a natural reaction for me, and I realized I did like her. I wasn't sure how that situation would work. I didn't really want to be responsible for her sobriety. Meaning she was fragile, and I didn't want to do some shit to make her mad or sad and have her going to get drunk or high because of it. Plus, she hadn't been sober long. What if she slipped back into her old ways and ended up taking a watch from me or some shit? I didn't want to judge her on her past, but according to her, she hadn't even been clean for three full months yet. That was very early.

The club closed, I finished up everything I had to do, and I met Liah at my car. Once we got inside, I looked over at her. "Until you tell me you're not mad at me anymore, I'm gon' bug the shit out of you. You don't even have to come back to work if you don't want. I'll pay your bills."

She let out a chuckle. "What?"

"I'm dead serious."

"It's cool Fahan. I'm not mad."

We drove to her apartment in an awkward silence that I didn't enjoy. We always had good conversation when we were in the car. Guess I fucked that up. Once I pulled up in front of her building, I stopped her from getting out of the car. "Talk to me."

"What was that kiss about? You always go around kissing fiends?"

I shut my car off, got out, and walked around to the passenger side. I opened the door and she got out. Once she was outside the car, I closed the door and pressed my body up against hers. "I kissed you because I'm feeling you. I guess I been feeling you. I'm sorry. I don't think either one of us are in the position to become emotionally attached to anyone, but I like you, and I value our friendship. I'm sorry."

Liah stared at me for a minute, and then she surprised the fuck out of me. She leaned into me and that time, she kissed me. Our tongues danced and my dick got hard again as we kissed in the parking lot of her apartment complex. Liah broke the kiss. "You want to come in?"

"You sure we should do that?"

She smiled. "I agree with you. We both don't need anything too heavy. I'm just horny as fuck. You started something by kissing me. Now finish it."

"Bet."

I followed her into her apartment. Inside, I followed her to her bedroom where she undressed. I picked her up and put her on her dresser. I buried my face in the crook of her neck and inhaled her scent. She smelled sweet. Out of all the women I had sex with after Dior, what I was doing with Liah felt different. I sucked on her neck, and she moaned.

My finger found her center, and I rubbed her clit gently as I sucked her neck. Liah's moans got louder until I covered my lips with hers and continued to stroke her. My mouth moved down to her breasts, and she started trembling and whimpering. I could tell that she came. I pulled a condom from my back pocket and undressed. Once the condom was on, I covered her lips with mine and put my dick in her. We both moaned as I began to move in and out of her. I sped up the pace, and she wrapped her arms around my neck.

I stared into her eyes. "What I gotta do to make you cum on this dick?"

"From the back," she panted.

I wasted no time easing out of her and pulling her off the dresser. I slid into her from behind, and she gripped the dresser as I moved in and out of her. "Fahan," she moaned my name in a sexy ass voice as she came and creamed all over the condom.

"Fucckk," I hissed as I moved in and out of her even faster. I bit my bottom lip as I stroked her pink, juicy walls. By the time I exploded into the condom, Liah had cum a third time.

"Damn," I panted, breathing hard as hell.

"Now you're almost forgiven."

"That's fair," I replied. I knew it was going to take some time for Liah to forgive me for what I said. I wasn't going to give up, but I respected that she'd need time. What I said was fucked up. Maybe seeing that nigga pouring liquor in her mouth got me in my feelings, and I needed to shake that shit off. I was having too much fun being single to be in another relationship anytime soon.

# 32

## AZAAN

I eyed Vickie with a hint of disgust on my face. "You got your shit together? 'Cus I don't mind keeping him."

It had been three weeks since I took Aheem from her. After we left Haiti, I took Aheem to visit his grandmother, and Vickie was there. She begged me to let her have Aheem back. the fact that he spent two whole weeks with me before she even called to check on him was unacceptable to me. I'd never known Vickie to be a deadbeat, but people changed.

"Yes Azaan. I was fucked up for a minute, but you know I love my son. I was just so mad at you, that I didn't want to dial your number. I know that's not an excuse, but I messed up. Going out and drinking and shit didn't numb the pain. I still missed my baby, and I want him back. No more clubbing for me or doing anything stupid. I just want to spend time with my son."

I knew my son loved his mom, so I didn't want to punish him by not letting him see her. Jayda said after she finished law school, she wouldn't be opposed to having a beach house in Miami. We decided that a nice compromise would be living in North Carolina half the year and Miami the other half. She also decided that since we were going to be back and forth between two states, it would make sense for her to have her own law firm versus working for someone else. She knew it was going to be a lot of hard work, but I had her back one hundred percent.

I said my good-byes to my son and went outside to leave. Fahan was waiting in the car so we could head back to North Carolina. We'd had a lot of fun in Haiti, but I was missing my baby. "So you know we generally don't keep secrets right?" Fahan asked when he backed out of the driveway.

I looked over at him. "Yeah, so what's good?"

He chuckled. "You probably gon' talk all types of shit, which is why I was debating on whether or not to tell you, but I fucked Liah."

"Ahhhhh shit," I groaned, and he laughed. She still wasn't my most favorite person in the world, but I was tied to Jayda now, and that was her sister. Plus, so far so good. I was just holding my breath waiting on her to fuck up and break Jayda's heart. I hoped it didn't happen though. Even with how I felt about her, I had to admit that cleaned up, she was a very pretty woman. She'd picked up a good twenty pounds, and she looked clean and healthy. It's almost hard to recall her when she was looking bad. I just hoped my brother knew what he was doing.

"We just keeping it light on some friend shit. We both agreed that a relationship or anything heavy isn't what we need right now. As long as she doesn't switch up on me, I'm fine."

"You're grown my man, and I trust your decisions. If you rocking, I'm rolling. Straight like that."

Fahan looked surprised that I didn't give him a lecture, but I was happy with life, and I was just letting shit go with the flow. The twins were kicking Jayda's ass, but my baby was handling it like a G. The club was doing well, and I was about to wrap it up with the pills. I made a lot of money selling drugs, and it was time for that chapter of my life to close. I had a million dollars in savings, and I was looking into other legal ventures, so I'd be straight.

Looking back on shit, I hated the way things ended with Vickie. She was my lady for a long time, and I never would have guessed that things would have gone so left for us. I truly believed though that I was supposed to be with Jayda. She had to lose Biggs, and I had to lose Vickie. I could only take that to mean that God had some really big plans for us, and I was here for it.

# 33

# DIOR

"**D**amn, this looks good. Thank you so much," I gushed as I looked at my reflection in the mirror.

A month after Nico's bitch ass cut me in the face, the cut had healed, but it left a scar. The scar wasn't too bad. I was kind of self-conscious about it, but the make-up girl that I had hired had it covered up perfectly. My new manager had gotten me a hosting job at a club in South Carolina. Since I was attacked, I hadn't been doing any club appearances, but I was getting those weekly checks in the mail. This job was paying me $3,500 so I hired a make-up girl and decided to stop sitting in the house moping. I wasn't even trying to get revenge on Nico. Fuck it. I maced him, he cut me, I was done with the shit. Since more shows were airing, my popularity was growing, and I was good. I still missed Fahan, but I fucked up. Life goes on, and since being on the show, mad niggas were in my DMs. A bitch was popping.

"You're welcome girl."

She collected her things to leave, and I looked at myself in the mirror. I was dressed in a red bodycon dress, and I was looking good, if I do say so myself. The door to the room that I was in opened, and in stepped Marshon. I had to bite the inside of my cheek to keep my mouth from falling open. He looked just that damn good. I had a few drinks, so I was feeling good, and I could tell by his low eyes that he felt good too. He came over and invaded my personal space.

"You still mad at me?"

"Yeap," I stated, trying to play tough, but my heart was beating like a bass drum. I remembered the sex that we had and how good it felt, and my entire body became flushed.

"Let me make it up to you," he stated before placing a juicy, wet kiss on my neck.

I stepped back from him as my pussy began to cream. "I have to go."

Marshon stepped forward and kissed me on the lips. "You can't leave with me tonight?"

I stared at his juicy, pussy eating lips. Shit, I was single and his dick was good, so why not? "I'll think about it."

Marshon smiled and we left the room. If Fahan didn't want me back, then that's what it was. A bitch was borderline famous, and I was about to be out here living my best single life.

## 34

## JAYDA

"You ready?" I asked Azaan with a smile.

"For sure."

"Okay." I took a deep breath and threw the ball down that I'd been holding. When it hit the concrete, it shattered, and pink dust flew out. Family members screamed because we knew that I was pregnant with at least one girl.

Azaan did exactly what I'd just done, and blue smoke came out of his. He picked me up and spun me around. I knew I was having fraternal twins because my babies had different sacks. That was a clue for me that they may be a different sex, but I wasn't sure. I was more than happy because I never wanted to be pregnant again. I couldn't wait to meet my babies, but I wanted my body back.

"You happy?" Azaan asked as he placed my feet on the ground.

"I'm very happy."

When I met Azaan, I was broken. I still couldn't understand why Biggs had been taken from me. I was going through life numb, but Azaan made me feel again. For as scared as I was to let him in, he was patient with me, and it was worth it. Who would have thought that him coming in to rent a car would have led to this? We went to interact with mostly my friends and family. Azaan and Fahan did fly their dad and sisters out for the gender reveal, and I met them.

I walked over to Liah who was fucking up her plate of food. "You good sis?"

"I am. Congratulations. So now I have two babies to keep me busy. Well, I will in four months."

"When you're not going out on dates," I teased. "I see how you and Fahan keep looking at each other too." I was so proud of Liah that she was still clean, and she'd even enrolled in school.

She laughed. "That's just my lil' cut buddy. We're cool. I don't need the pressure of a relationship."

"I can dig it. As long as you're happy."

"I am."

Her smile was genuine, and I could tell that she was really happy, and so was I. I was more than happy. Life was perfect.

THE END.

Author note: If you read my books regularly, then you know for the most part, I like to wrap my series up in two parts when possible. Being that Fahan was locked up most of the book, his story didn't take off until the end, but I wasn't too pressed because after all, the cover says, Azaan and Jayda. This story ended at almost 68,000 words, and even if I would have ended it at 100,000 some would still feel that his story ended too soon. So, if you guys want Fahan to get his own story, I will be more than glad to do that. Also, you know I stay working, and I'm pleased to announce that Southern Thugs Do It Better is getting a prequel. Enjoy this sneak peek.

## 35

# ALEXIS

I grabbed a pair of Seven's jeans to toss into the washer. As I always did, I reached inside each pocket to remove anything that may have been left behind. I'd been doing my man's laundry for the past year since we'd been living together. In all the times that I'd done his laundry, I hadn't found anything, but still I checked. It was something my mother taught me to do when she first taught me to do laundry. My eyes narrowed into slits as my hand hit something. From the texture of the item, I didn't even have to see it to be able to surmise what it was that'd I'd located, but I pulled it out anyway.

My breath caught in my throat at the sight of the shiny, gold Magnum wrapper. My man had a condom in his pocket, and we didn't use those. Hadn't used those in a minute, so why the fuck did he have one in his pocket? Seven was a hustler, and he kept late nights. Some mornings, he got up early, but some days, he chose to sleep until around noon. Today was one of the days that he chose to sleep in, but I was about to wake his ass up. He had me fucked all the way up. Cheating ass bastard. I tossed the jeans onto the floor and stormed to our bedroom with condom in hand.

"Seven," I roared, knowing it would probably take more than that to wake his tired ass up, and he was for sure tired in more ways than one. He didn't even stir. "Seven, get up!" I put as much bass in my voice as I could.

Finally, he stirred. Opening his eyes, he looked over at me. "Why the fuck you yelling bruh?" His voice was raspy and sleep filled.

"Why the fuck you got condoms in your pocket?" I roared. I'd been in quite a few shitty relationships before meeting Seven. He was unlike any other man that I'd ever been with. He was refreshing, and I loved him. To know that he was cheating on me made it feel as if a million daggers had penetrated my heart. I didn't want to believe it. I was hurt, and I was pissed, and he was 'bout to feel me.

"Fuck you talking 'bout?" he asked with a scowl on his face as he sat up and looked over at me.

I tossed the condom at him and it hit him in the eye. He wasn't pleased. "Chill the fuck out," he barked as if he was in the position to be demanding shit.

I spoke slowly so that his dumb ass would get it. "I was doing your bitch ass laundry the way that I always do, and I found a condom in the pock-etttttt," I dragged out the last word.

The fog finally cleared from Seven's brain, and he comprehended what I was saying. He looked up at me trying to play it cool, but I could tell from the look in his eyes that he was panicking on the inside. I wasn't sure if Seven had ever cheated on me before, but if he had, he must have gotten too comfortable because a condom in his pocket was just messy. I wasn't even the type to go through his phone or to clock his every move. Him getting caught was just stupidity plain and simple, and I was about to tear into his stupid ass. His light brown eyes held a hint of fear as he tossed the covers off his body.

"Chill man, I don't know where that shit came from. Maybe Emir left it in my car or something and I picked it up and forgot to get rid of it." The lie rolled off his tongue.

I scoffed. It's no secret that his friend Emir cheated on my sister Janai. It was no secret at all, but Seven was still a fuck boy for throwing his friend under the bus. I knew him and had Emir really left that condom in the car, Seven would have called and spazzed on him and tossèd it out the window. He was really trying to insult my intelligence, and that was pissing me off even more. I was heartbroken and frustrated. This was the very reason why I hesitated to move in with Seven. I knew that if shit ever hit the fan and we broke up, I'd have to be worried about where I would live. I didn't want to go back to my parents' house, and I for damn sure didn't want to stay with my sister and Emir.

"I hope she was worth it. I swear to God I hope she was worth it, because we're done," I declared as tears filled my eyes. As much as I loved Seven, I refused to be one of those girls. Why couldn't men just keep their dicks in their pants?

Seven stood up. "Man chill out talking 'bout we're done. You found a condom. It's not open, so clearly I didn't use it."

I rushed towards him and pushed him as hard as I could in the chest. "Stop trying to play me like I'm stupid! Three come in a box dummy. Maybe you bought a box and used two, threw the box away and stuck that one in your pocket which was dumb as fuck. You're not a broke nigga. You could have thrown that one away with the box and just bought some more the next time you wanted to fuck the hoe. Being cheap got you caught." I smirked.

Seven let out a defeated sigh. "You think you got all the sense. You act like you got it all figured out, but you don't. I didn't cheat on you."

"Take the passcode off your phone and let me look through it," I demanded. That was something that I had never done. Once again, there it was, panic.

"You tripping for real this morning. What, your dot 'bout to come on or something?" Instead of calling my monthly cycle a period, Seven called it a dot. Don't ask me why.

I sucked my teeth and clenched my fists at my sides. "I'm trying really hard to keep my hands to myself because no matter how stupid you are, domestic violence isn't cool, but baby I swear you trying me," I yelled.

"You will not make me think I'm crazy. You fucked up, not me." I pointed my finger at him. "I'm out this bitch."

I headed towards the closet and began pulling my clothes from the hangers while Seven stood there looking stupid. "You're really jumping the gun. I didn't cheat on you. How you just gon' leave me like that?"

I didn't respond to him as I grabbed my suitcase. The house I shared with him was my home. Now, I had to be homeless because he cheated. That's why my daddy always told me you shouldn't play house. Seven spoiled me, and he paid all of the bills. I had money of my own, but the house was his. He was living in it alone when we met, so I couldn't exactly make him get out. As bad as I hated to have to go to a hotel, I refused to stay just because I didn't want to be inconvenienced. Before Seven, I was in a terrible relationship, and I swore to myself that I'd never allow myself to be mistreated again. Cheating and any kind of abuse, be it mental or physical, were all grounds for me to dismiss a nigga quick.

Seven just stood there watching me as I filled the suitcase to capacity. Once I zipped it shut, he walked over to me. "Please don't leave me Alexis. We're better than this. We can't just sit down and talk?"

"Nope," I stated and went to grab my things from the bathroom. He was guilty because even though he was begging me not to go, if he was truly innocent, he would have been acting an ass. He would have been defending himself way harder, but deep down he knew he messed up. Plus, the nigga couldn't even let me look through his phone. That told me everything that I needed to know.

I wondered just how long he'd been cheating on my dumb ass. As I grabbed my toothbrush, lotion, and other personal hygiene items, I wondered how many women there had been. God, I was so stupid.

# ABOUT THE AUTHOR

Natisha Raynor discovered her love for reading in third grade. As she got older she preferred being in her bedroom reading a good book versus playing outside. Natisha began writing her own stories at 12 years old, when the books she was reading no longer held her interest. Natisha wrote for fun for many years until she reached her mid-twenties and sought out a publishing deal. In 2015 she self-published her first novel and since then she's penned more than thirty books. Natisha resides in Raleigh, North Carolina with her two teenaged children.

### *Stay Connected:*
If you haven't already joined my reading group, please do so: My Heart Beats Books

facebook.com/Natisha-Raynor-Presents-1003152116362757

instagram.com/author_natisha_raynor

## ALSO BY NATISHA RAYNOR

Idris and Wisdom: The Most Savage Summer Ever (3 book series)

Cherished by a Thug (2-Book series)

In Love with the King of North Carolina (3 book series)

Shawty got a Thang for them Country Boys (3 book series)

Married to a Haitian Mob Boss (2 book series)

A Gangsta and His Shawty: Heirs to the Baptiste Throne (2 book series)

For the Love of You

In Love with the Hood in Him (2 book series)

Aashiem and Hysia: A Dope Boy Love Story

A'san and Bishop: A Thug's Obsession

When Love is Stronger than Pride

Torn Between A Boss And A Real One (2 book series)

She's Got A Thug In His Feelings (2 book series)

Fallin' For A Carolina Menace (2 book series)

Southern Thugs Do It Better (3 book series)

She Made A Savage Change His Ways(2 book series)

For my full catalog check out my

Amazon Author Page

**Royalty Publishing House** is now accepting manuscripts from aspiring or experienced urban romance authors!

## WHAT MAY PLACE YOU ABOVE THE REST:

Heroes who are the ultimate book bae: strong-willed, maybe a little rough around the edges but willing to risk it all for the woman he loves.

Heroines who are the ultimate match: the girl next door type, not perfect - has her faults but is still a decent person. One who is willing to risk it all for the man she loves.

The rest is up to you! Just be creative, think out of the box, keep it sexy and intriguing!

If you'd like to join the Royal family, send us the first 15K words (60 pages) of your completed manuscript to submissions@royaltypublishing-house.com

# LIKE OUR PAGE!

Be sure to <u>LIKE</u> our Royalty Publishing House page on Facebook!

CPSIA information can be obtained
at www.ICGtesting.com
Printed in the USA
LVHW021502090819
627129LV00002B/311/P